COLLATERAL

BENSON FIRST RESPONDERS
BOOK 3

LISA PHILLIPS

TWO DOGS PUBLISHING, LLC.

eBook ISBN: 979-8-88552-160-4

Paperback ISBN: 979-8-88552-161-1

Published by Two Dogs Publishing, LLC. Idaho, USA

Cover Design by Sasha Almazan and Gene Mollica, GS Cover Design Studio, LLC

Edited by Christy Callahan, Professional Publishing Services

Audiobook published by Recorded Books

ONE

London pulled the car into the garage and parked it beside the Jag. Every time he saw that thing, he wanted to punch Phoenix in his smug face. One day he would get a sledgehammer and go all Carrie Underwood on it.

London parked the car. Beside him in the passenger seat, Rio gripped the top of the backpack, twisting it in his hands.

"Job's done. What's going on?" London didn't get out.

Rio said nothing.

"Dude, you're gonna get cold feet now? You a coward?"

Rio shot him a look, then shoved open the door.

London grabbed his arm, shoving him up against the wall by the freezer. "You gonna ruin this?" He put pressure on Rio's neck. "Tell me, so I can kill you now."

Rio said nothing.

"Are you?"

He choked out one word, "No."

London stared into his eyes for a second, then pushed off Rio and went inside.

London held the door for a long second so the guy behind

him could enter. "It's done." When he'd caught it, London headed into the kitchen. "Did ya hear me?"

"I heard you." Berlin stood over the breakfast bar, schematics on the table in front of him.

London figured he had. For once the music coming from the stereo wired through the whole house was playing low. The kitchen smelled like last night's dinner, underlaid with the constant, slightly musty smell of being between house-keepers.

Berlin lifted a mug and sipped while he studied the paper he'd rolled out before putting little gold Scottie dog statues on the corners as paperweights.

London dumped the keys to the Porsche on the counter by the coffee pot and poured himself a mug.

The guy behind him breezed by. "Berlin."

London lifted his head. "Rio."

Rio got a beer from the fridge and chugged down half of it. "Where's everyone else?"

Berlin pointed with a finger toward the living room that led out onto an expansive back porch with a hot tub and a view of the pool, then the mountains.

London put cream in his coffee. "Did Miami wake up?"

Berlin shook his head.

Rio headed for the living room, pulling off his shirt, so he was just in basketball shorts. He only wore a shirt when they left the house, and even that didn't always guarantee he'd be fully clothed. It was the brand he'd cultivated, and it worked for him.

London turned to Berlin. "What about Phoenix?" Miami had been asleep on the pool table when London and Rio left a couple of hours ago.

"In the hot tub with Shara." Berlin didn't give away an ounce of how he felt about that. "No one saw you?"

London lowered the mug from his mouth. "Of course not. It all went smoothly, just like you said."

Berlin nodded.

"We're still on track for tomorrow?"

"Day after." Berlin looked up. "Just to be sure."

"Copy that." London took a sip of his coffee. "You know we'll be good. The team is tight."

They made sure nothing would go wrong. Between Berlin's planning and the skill each of them brought, they hadn't failed yet. They studied afterward and fixed their mistakes. They'd started out good. Now they were great.

Berlin still pushed them.

Good. They didn't need to get cocky, even if Phoenix built his brand on that. They couldn't assume nothing would go wrong. The minute they did that, they were done either way.

Dead, or in jail.

London wasn't gonna let that happen.

Something crashed then shattered in the living room. Berlin headed there first. London jogged behind him to where Rio had pulled Phoenix out of the hot tub and now had him shoved against the wall with an arm to his throat.

Berlin roared, "What's going on?"

London headed for the hot tub. The back patio doors had been slid all the way open so they were now folded. Pushed against the wall so the patio and inside living room were one big room now. He held out his hand to Shara.

She whimpered but grabbed his hand.

As he hauled her out of the hot tub, he said, "Go get dressed," his voice low.

She scurried through the room, dripping water as she went.

"She was mine last night!" Rio yelled the words in Phoenix's face. "But you can't stand to lose, can you?"

"It's how I play the game, dude." Phoenix's bright blue eyes flashed.

"Back off of Shara." Rio glared.

"Both of you back off." Berlin held up his hands. "Focus up, everyone. We have a meeting in twenty, so get cleaned up."

London winced. Berlin's "meetings" usually meant at least one of them wound up bloody. It made them all better at what they did, so no one complained during.

Just after.

He headed for the pool table, where Miami lay stretched out, still asleep despite all the noise, and shook his shoulder. "Get up, bro. Meeting in twenty."

TWO

"Someone in your predicament shouldn't be so cocky." Clare Juarez, owner and CEO of Vanguard Investigations, stood over the woman in the chair.

Selena struggled against the zip ties holding her hands together and her elbows to the chair. Her feet weren't tied. Clare was an exacting taskmaster, but she wasn't mean.

Clare studied the bound woman, watching for intention in her movement. The bite of her lower lip. The flicker of a frown on her forehead.

Selena tipped the chair backward.

"Don't fall back if your hands are tied behind your back. You can break your fingers or wrists. Or even dislocate a shoulder." Clare should know since her trigger finger still clicked sometimes. "Nearly got it?"

"I'm not gonna dislocate my thumb just to get out."

"And I'm not gonna assume you might have a blade hidden on you somewhere. You could get searched."

Selena grunted. "Kidnappers feeling me up. Sounds great." She sucked in a breath. "I almost got it." The frown on her forehead deepened.

Clare resisted the urge to circle the chair and see if Selena was right. Instead, she glanced over at the grunting from the room's far end. Two of her employees were sparring in the raised boxing ring with no pads and no gloves. Mostly they seemed to be content trash-talking each other and then using elbows and knees.

The whole place smelled like sweat. Usually music pumped loudly through the expensive stereo system she'd had installed, but not this morning. The early crowd favored earbuds, using the wall of windows to assess their form as they lifted free weights.

In the mirror she spotted someone come through the door behind her.

Peter Olson strode in with an iPad and headed right for her, skirting around the edge of the crash pads so he didn't walk on them in his boots. The twenty-one-year-old wore cargos and a black polo with the Vanguard logo on it, and he'd filled out in the last few months while his twin brother, Simon, who worked more in the office on his computer, remained more slender.

Selena still hadn't removed the ropes securing her to the chair.

Clare turned as he approached. The day she'd begun hiring employees old enough to be her children was the day she'd felt old for the first time. Too many pangs of her past resonated pain in her chest—whether she liked it or not.

Long time ago.

She'd experienced plenty of pain since then. Like losing Selena's mother, Kara, which meant she took the girl in and now did everything she could to protect Kara's daughter.

There were plenty more recent things she could worry about. Like making sure Selena could take care of herself—no matter what. Clare had a ledger of things to make up for.

"Got a minute?" Peter's gaze skated through Selena, who basically ignored him. "Having fun?"

She blew out a breath that ruffled the hair on her forehead. "Don't distract me."

Clare figured Selena and Peter might be a good match in how competitive they were. Then again, they would make an explosive combination. Good thing neither of them had realized the other one seemed interested. And Selena insisted on sticking it out with her boyfriend.

Clare asked him, "What do you have?"

He flicked the hair off his face. "That cold case you assigned us last week."

"Already?"

He nodded. "I figured you'd want to know. Davis and I got back late last night. We have everything ready for—"

Clare heard a note in his tone. Spotted the slight flinch—a warning of what was coming. For her.

"—you."

Selena slammed into Clare, knocking her off her feet. Clare twisted in the air so she landed flat on her back and kept her chin tucked, Selena's head out of the way so they didn't crack skulls. Her back hit the floor. Clare didn't even let Selena take a breath.

She wrapped her legs in the young woman's, only hearing her skirt rip a little as she flipped Selena onto her back.

Selena yelped.

Clare reached for the young woman's hands. Selena pulled one out of Clare's grasp, just like she'd taught her. "Good."

"Note I'm not head-butting you, but I could."

Clare grinned. "I'm not choking you out."

"Much obliged." Selena kicked with her legs in a move

that should've flipped Clare over her head. But Clare taught her that as well. "Dang it."

Clare chuckled. "Do you yield?"

"Do *you*?"

The sparring partners had quit their game and come over to see what was happening. Selena got a leg wrapped around Clare's. They started to go, but Clare planted a hand and refused to let Selena topple her. She wound her arm around Selena's back, grabbed the pocket on her hip, and flipped the younger woman onto her face, one-handed.

Someone whooped.

Selena expelled a breath against the crash mat. "That was good. I wanna learn that move."

Clare pulled one of her hands up between her shoulder blades. "Do you concede now?"

"Fine." Selena grunted as Clare let go and helped her stand. "I'll get you one day."

Clare nodded. "Yes, you probably will."

"I got out of the chair." Selena grinned. Her phone chimed with a new text, then two more right after it. "Gotta go. Alex is ready to go to breakfast."

Clare kept her mouth shut about Selena's boyfriend and how he had her at his beck and call.

Selena gave her a quick hug. "Laters."

"Bye, hon." Clare watched her go, then turned to Peter. The sparring partners had wandered off.

Peter had a look on his face.

"What?"

His expression shuttered. "Nothing. Wanna look at the file?"

"Yes." They walked together to where she'd left her heels, then to the elevator and up to the office level. Cold Cases on the floor below. Her office was at the end of the hall, and she had a back door up to an apartment most people didn't know she had on the top floor, above the safe house apartments. Floors between housed other departments. Supplies— and the undercover closet. "I appreciate you not mentioning it in front of Selena."

"When will you tell her you're looking into her father's disappearance?"

Clare gave her assistant a little wave, motioning with a finger. Lena nodded. "Probably around the time there's an answer to give her, rather than a whole lot of questions she's already got." Clare checked her appearance in the mirror by her credenza. She smoothed down her hair before she sat behind her desk and slid the chair in. Her keyboard was covered with missed call notes Lena had left. It was going to be a busy day.

Peter stood in front of her desk. "You're determined to find him?"

The young man had changed a lot since she hired him after he and his twin brother had completed their community service hours with her company. No way was she going to let talent like that go to waste—or get corrupted by a man like their late father, who'd been determined to see them come under his wing.

The twins had been smart enough to steer clear of him.

Now she was honing those instincts and putting the skills they already had to good use. Peter was now training under Bob Davis—another man she'd hired while on probation. While Simon practically ran her cyber division.

"Why don't you let me know what you found?" She settled back in her chair. "Then I'll know if it's even possible."

Teaching the girl to take care of herself was only part of it. Much like with the business Clare ran, there were moving parts.

The end all amounted to one thing, though.

She would finally feel like she'd made amends for the things she'd done.

Peter handed her the file and sat. "Davis found the sheriff at the time of Selena's father's disappearance. He had old files in his garage he'd forgotten about. The case file was tucked away."

Clare opened the file, determined to reopen this case. "Talk me thorough it."

THREE

Lieutenant Gage Deluca surveyed the street. Just another flop house in another rundown neighborhood. Was the missing girl here?

Sergeant Liam O'Connell pulled the SWAT van over to the side of the street where the targets in the house wouldn't be able to see them.

Piled in the back were three officers, the five of them in matching black cargo uniforms. Bulletproof vests. Helmets. They jumped out and huddled on the sidewalk. "We've run this a hundred times." They'd been working together nearly four years. "Let's do it clean."

Gage turned to lead the way down the cracked sidewalk, past an overgrown lawn. A rottweiler behind a chain-link fence stared at them as they passed. Growled. Gage left him to it, not wanting to get tangled in a war over who was alpha here.

"Let's go." He needed his three officers to speed up, not amble each other into being slower and slower. Generally they goaded one another and wound up tussling like siblings.

The one upmanship worked great when they directed that energy at the job. The task at hand.

They won, it meant he won.

Success meant he secured his spot as the new SWAT lieutenant in Benson PD. Gage wasn't going to accept anything else.

"White house?" Dakota Masterson called from behind them.

A quick glance told Gage he was right about Officer Masterson's condition. Glassy eyes. Flushed cheeks. That twitchy thing he did. Six months ago he'd been in a car accident.

"Lieutenant?"

Gage answered Officer Blake Reed's non-question. "Take your positions."

Dakota headed first down the side of the house. Jasper Hollingsworth, whose father was a Washington State senator, followed.

Blake went the other direction down the side of the house. They'd radio in if they found a side window access, or a door inside. Or they'd convene on the back patio and enter from there.

He and his sergeant would take the front.

Liam, his driver and best friend since the first day of police academy, glanced over. His Irish heritage showed in those ice-blue eyes and blond hair. "He's bad today."

Gage didn't want to get distracted from the operation when they could figure out the long-term issue of Dakota and whatever he'd gotten into after it was done. Mission success came first, before anything else. Then he'd hammer Dakota with some reality and get him straightened out.

It wasn't anything they hadn't dealt with before as a team, but now Gage was lead things were different.

"Three and Four in position," Jasper called in.

"Five up." Blake had found an entry point, while Jasper had Dakota with him.

Gage grabbed the button for his radio. "One and two up." Liam nodded, squaring up to the front door. "Breach."

Liam kicked the front door in, and Gage went first. He stepped left, and Liam came in behind him. They swept the front living area. Or what was likely supposed to be that. The whole place was pretty much empty. Decorated in graffiti and holes in the walls where someone had punched or kicked at the drywall. There was a smear of blood about face height in the hallway.

"Forensics?" Liam followed, his focus on the room not the evidence despite his question.

Gage split left and joined Dakota in the kitchen, where the guy was gagging over the sink. "Later. Though Masterson just contaminated anything."

"Sorry." Dakota straightened, his face so pale his lips were skin color. The redhead from Idaho looked like he was about to pass out.

"Go outside, Officer Masterson. Get some air and call in the K-9 unit."

Dakota frowned. "Why?"

Because I'm your lieutenant. "Just do it." Gage passed him, leaving Liam to get the guy outside.

Reed stood in the dining area. "Crawlspace, no basement. No upstairs. Single level. Attic might have something in it."

Gage wasn't sure. He glanced between Jasper and Blake, the senator's son and the kid from the streets. Now they both bled blue and wore the same uniform. Brothers in a way life never would have offered them. "Figure out what this empty space is."

Jasper spun, his freshly styled dark-brown hair probably

cost more to get cut than Gage spent in a year on hair trims. "What empty space?"

"There's no garage." Gage pointed at the wall. "So what's between this and the front of the house?"

Blake grinned. "K-9?"

"Or demolition. But we have no probable cause to start ripping out walls. We only know Alberto was seen entering. There's no evidence the missing girl was here."

"About that..." Sergeant O'Connell strode in, blue material in his hand.

"Where'd you find that, Lee?" Blake took it and held the blue up. A woman's shirt. "Same one she was wearing when she was nabbed."

Gage looked at Liam. Sergeant O'Connell enjoyed police work, but a missing woman birthed an anger in him that Gage didn't like the look of right now. "Where's my K-9?"

"Across town." Liam shook his head. "Says he'd be half an hour after he wraps up the call he's on."

"Great." Gage didn't want to wait that long. Especially not if the victim was in the house.

Jasper looked at the wall, then ducked and looked inside the fireplace. Tilted his head and glanced up the chimney. When he said nothing, Gage figured he hadn't found the vic stuffed up there. Jasper straightened. "The fire department could get us through the wall."

"So can my boot." Liam headed for the wall beside the fire.

Blake snorted. "Mine, too, Sarge—I mean, Lieutenant."

Given Gage had been in the rank a few weeks, he let that go. "See what you can do, Reed. Jasper, go outside and check on Dakota."

"Copy that." Jasper touched his hair on the way by. "Wouldn't wanna get dust in my hair gel."

Gage grinned. The guy didn't actually care—they'd all seen him go toe-to-toe with a bus full of hockey players in a rainstorm and wound up covered in mud in five minutes—but he wanted them to think it was about the mess and his hair. Instead, it was about checking on their friend. "Don't let him sit in the truck!"

They would pull it closer to the house and call their captain. Let him know what they were doing. Gage wanted a result so they could tell the captain they actually found something. Otherwise Gage was going to get a chewing out for going off on a hunch.

He didn't care as much about losing the leader spot as he did about the simple fact it would mean the team was split up.

"Check this out." Liam spread his fingers on the wall, just above where a thin rail of trim split the bottom half from the top. "Nope. I thought I had it."

Gage studied the bottom half. "You do." He shooed the sergeant out of the way and pressed his hands against the lower part of the wall. It clicked and popped out. "On me."

They covered him. Gage had to crawl through the opening. Inside was barely bigger than a closet. He clicked the flashlight on his rifle and shined it around. Found the missing girl, curled up in the corner.

A hefty figure clipped his shoulder on the way to the opening. Gage stuck out his foot and tripped the guy. He slammed his head on the top lip of the hatch and slumped to the floor with a thud.

"Got 'im." Blake crouched to peer through the opening. "We're gonna go get lunch if you've got this covered."

Gage said, "She's in here."

He ignored the stale smell, and the dirty mattress against one wall, and crouched beside the girl. Gage touched two fingers to her throat, checking for a pulse, then keyed his mic. "Get an ambulance. She's alive."

FOUR

"Thank you." Clare strode past Russ Franklin's assistant and into the Benson PD Commissioner's office. "This place suits you, Russ."

The former US marshal sat behind the desk in an office decorated in wood and brass, complete with leather chairs. Muted light shined through the windows, the sky outside gray and overcast like it so often was in the Pacific Northwest—and the United Kingdom. She'd spent a stint at a base in England, and much preferred blue skies to dreary days and drizzling rain.

He grunted and removed his glasses. Rather than wearing a suit, which would have made him look like a mobster, he wore tan slacks and a buttoned gray-and-blue shirt. He hadn't shaved. He pushed back his chair and rounded his desk. "Hey, kid."

As he opened his arms, she stepped in for a quick squeeze. "Hey, yourself." She caught a whiff of cigar, which meant he had a lot going on and felt the need to sit on his back deck and spend some time thinking. That wasn't how she processed, but she understood feeling the same urge. The file Peter had

given her—the original police report of Selena's father's disappearance— offered her more questions and little in the way of
answers. The sheriff didn't remember the case, and the
deputy who'd written the report had died in a car accident
years later.

He leaned back, the crinkles around his eyes deepening.
"How's your mom?"

"Still kicking butt and taking names as Seattle's most
cutthroat criminal attorney."

"Of course she is." Russ chuckled.

"How's Addie?" Clare asked. "I haven't gotten into the
FBI office lately." Never mind that she didn't want to, and no
intention of doing so anytime soon.

Addie Franklin, the FBI Special Agent who ran the
Benson satellite office, had married a local photographer but
kept her maiden name for her professional life. Clare didn't
know if it helped or hindered her that her uncle was now the
police commissioner. Maybe it made her inroads with the PD.

"FBI and Benson Intelligence division are chasing a
domestic terror case," he said.

"Out of town?"

Russ motioned her to a seat and took his own behind the
desk. Behind him rows of leather-bound volumes were
flanked by petrified wood bookends. "They should have it all
wrapped up soon enough."

Clare nodded. "I have a fully equipped cyber division as
well as a full forensics lab staffed with the best people I could
hire and state-of-the-art equipment." She didn't want to make
it sound like the PD needed her help. "If it might help to have
any evidence processed faster than the lab here is able."

"You know they're backlogged. Everyone is backlogged."

"Vanguard is available. That's actually what I wanted to
talk to you about." She'd set this meeting weeks ago.

The next step for solidifying Vanguard in the community was to secure contracts with the local police or federal law enforcement. She couldn't bring herself to approach the FBI here—yet. She would, eventually but it was too raw right now. She wanted to start with the police anyway. Their department was a whole lot bigger than the four special agents in town and the tiny office they worked out of.

"Vanguard will bring all our professionalism and training to this." Clare sat a little straighter. "We're ready to help."

Russ stared at her with that steady gaze. "Why?"

"Because we live here. We might not be cops, but we want to make Benson better."

"Some of you are," he said. "Or *were*."

Clare swallowed. She'd expected that.

"Cops who are then required to hand over evidence to Vanguard might see it as an integrity issue that you have staff on your payroll who are convicted criminals."

"I believe you'll find they are rehabilitated criminals." Clare paused. "Or do you not believe the justice system works?"

Russ grinned.

The police department loved their gruff former marshal commissioner. He was their gatekeeper. Which she respected, except for the fact the point was to keep out people like her. Just because she had a guy in her cold case division who happened to have been a dirty cop—but was also the father of Stella Davis, one of the FBI agents in town, whose husband was a BPD detective. Among others, like Peter and Simon, the twins she'd hired once they completed their community service.

"I hire the best. I stand behind them one hundred percent."

Russ stared for a second, then slid over a file and flipped it open. "The feds can't take this case because it's not federal. Yet, at least."

"And as soon as it is, they'll swoop in and take it from you?"

"Let's try and keep that from happening."

Clare had no stake in it, but she understood the friendly rivalry. After all, she'd been army for years. The military thrived on competition.

"There have been three robberies in the last few weeks," he began. "One local check cashing place, a money transfer store, and a storage unit that has a highly secure annex for safety deposit boxes. All three were hit by a crew of five guys who got in and out fast." He handed her the file.

"Evidence?"

"Not much to speak of. They know what they're doing, disarming security. But there's no pattern to it. Each business had completely unique systems in place to keep their assets secure. Face value, it makes no sense why they'd hit these places."

And the FBI and Benson Intelligence were both busy on a high-profile case. Meanwhile, if Vanguard proved key in bringing down a crew of thieves, it would solidify their standing in the community as a reputable company who worked with the police. On the other hand, if they failed? Clare didn't want to think about that.

"So far they haven't crossed state lines or hit anywhere backed federally."

"Doesn't mean it won't escalate that direction." Clare studied the police reports. The lack of a pattern was curious, until she put together the sequence and realized it pointed to one thing. She pulled out her phone, but then decided to just call into the office as soon as she left here. "Can I take this?" She waved the police file.

Russ nodded. "Keep me apprised of anything. I want daily updates."

"Of course." Clare stood, already headed for the door.

"Don't let me down."

She turned at the door, surety settling in her in a way she liked a lot. They weren't going to fail. "Vanguard has got this."

Clare headed for the stairs, just to burn off some of the energy now moving through her. She didn't need to get over-loaded and then crash. She reached the ground floor and opted to go through the lobby, since the FBI was out on a case.

The front hall buzzed, a wall of glass windows on one side so she could see into the police department central precinct. The sergeant on the front desk lifted his chin. Clare did the same in reply.

On the other side of the hall, opposite the PD, was the tiny office for the FBI. Barely a conference table and a few desks. A lone woman worked their reception desk, just inside the door—someone Clare had never met.

She stopped in the hall in front of the picture hanging there. A memorial to FBI Special Agent Kyle Averson, killed nearly a year ago. He hadn't even been in town long. Just long enough to start to like it here—even though he said otherwise. They'd joked about that over lunch. He'd asked her to dinner, and she'd begun to have real feelings for him.

Then he'd been killed.

The door at the end of the hall opened, and a group of cops with SWAT on their vests strode in, talking and joking with each other. Clare studied the image of Kyle. *I'm sorry.*

There hadn't been enough of something to claim there had been much of anything between them. Tell that to Clare's heart. Loss was loss.

She started to turn and someone clipped her shoulder.

"Sorry, ma'am."

He had a nice voice, but she'd been fooled by that before.

Clare waved a hand and kept going toward the front doors. Out into the daylight. There was no point dwelling on the past.

Not when there was a case to solve.

Clare pulled out her phone. "It's me. Find me a bank in town with these three parameters."

FIVE

Gage pulled out his chair and sat. On his keyboard someone had left a note. His mom's landlord had called—again—asking when he'd clear her stuff out of the house. Plus a bunch of stuff about condolences for his loss. Gage had paid two months of rent, so technically he still had two weeks to figure out clearing out her stuff. The guy probably just wanted to raise the rent with a new tenant.

He crumpled the paper and tossed it into the tiny wastepaper basket by his desk.

God, it doesn't have to hurt like this. But it does.

He'd become a believer a few weeks ago. He was still waiting for his life to get easier.

Someone knocked on the door to the office all the guys shared. Five desks shoved into one conference room, and he was the only one here. The only difference between this and four months ago was that he now occupied the lieutenant's desk instead of the sergeant's.

They had the basement of the police building to themselves, and that was fine. Like the fact the entire PD pretty much called the SWAT department "the cave." Didn't matter. They liked it down here.

Gage got a look at who was at the door and shot to his feet. "Captain."

McCauley's features warmed. "Lieutenant Deluca." He came over and held out his hand and they shook. Dennis McCauley, the Captain over the detectives division, settled on the edge of Blake's desk—probably because it was the cleanest. "Just wanted to drop by and offer my congratulations on a job well done this morning."

"I'm just getting ready to write up the report now."

Captain McCauley nodded. "I heard all about it from your captain. Says you boys did a good job finding that girl and her captor in that flop house. But he wasn't too clear on how you knew she'd be there."

Gage wanted to wince but hoped the expression didn't bleed onto his face. "Just a hunch, really."

"Well, it paid off. Like all good hunches."

"Yes, sir." He wondered if McCauley was going to ask if they had the homeowner's permission to kick the door in. Fact was, the corporation had emailed back with the go ahead to do what they needed to do. They were between tenants, and whoever occupied the place had been squatting illegally.

"Nice work, Lieutenant Deluca." McCauley held out his hand. "You boys keep it up."

"Yes, sir."

"My door is always open." McCauley trailed out.

Gage exhaled a long breath.

"Speaking of close ones." Liam strode in, shoving Dakota in front of him, before Gage even had a second to figure out what that visit from the police chief meant.

"Yes, Sergeant?" Better to start off on official terms, rather than as the friends they also were. The whole team felt like the brothers he'd never had, and the same would be true even if there was a sister on the team. Siblings who worked together. So long as they understood he was the one in charge. He'd take responsibility for anything that happened because it *was* his responsibility.

"Dakota wants to talk to you." Liam tugged Dakota down into a chair and rolled him toward Gage.

Dakota twisted to look at his sergeant. "Lee, this is ridiculous. You're making something out of nothing."

"SWAT trained snipers don't get shaky hands and drop a cup of coffee." Liam folded his arms.

"Look, Gage..." Dakota rang his hands together.

"It's 'Lieutenant.'" Gage sat back in his chair. Dakota's history pointed to exactly one thing, and it was no good for him or the team. Anything Gage ordered went on his personnel file. It would always be there. Unless Dakota could handle it himself.

"So you're gonna be like that?" Dakota glanced back at Liam. "And you, *Sarge*? I thought we were cool."

"We were," Liam said. "Until you jeopardize our lives and this team."

Before Dakota could argue further, Gage said, "So what are you going to do about it?"

"I can handle it." Dakota shifted to sit up straighter in his chair. "I can."

"What's going on? Because you know we can help," Gage said. "We've got your back, no matter what."

Dakota scratched at the hair over his ear, longer than his normal cut and dirty like he needed a shower. "Kyla broke up with me."

Gage blew out a breath. "Sorry, bro. I know you really liked her."

Dakota made a face. He was trying to be mad more than

heartbroken, and Gage didn't blame him. "She moved to Eugene. Said she likes it better, and her mom lives there." He shrugged.

Gage nodded. "I know what it's like when the woman you love leaves." That was a long time ago now, and the situation had been a whole lot more complicated, but the particulars stood. "But if there's something you need to deal with, we want to help."

Before he could say more the alarm on the wall erupted into that tinny buzz, signaling a callout. "SWAT response requested. Union Street, First National Bank of Benson. Armed robbery in progress, possible hostage situation."

"I got it." Liam grabbed the radio on his belt and called in they were mobilizing so the dispatcher would mark them as responding.

Gage stood and held out his hand. Dakota clasped his wrist and Gage pulled him to his feet. "Let's go, Masterson."

"On your six, *Lieutenant*."

Gage didn't totally love the tone of that, but there wasn't time to worry about it. The north end of the cave had a garage bay that led out onto a ramp up to the street. They pulled out a minute later, and Liam flipped on lights and sirens.

"Shouldn't take us long to get there." Gage didn't even bother pulling up a map. They all knew the bank on Union Street in the middle of downtown.

Blake leaned between the two front seats. "Lieutenant, when are you gonna let me drive?"

Gage glanced over and saw his friend was at least partially serious.

Liam gripped the big steering wheel. "When you're hauling my cold, dead body back from a callout."

Gage blinked. "Bro."

"Fine. But it stands." Liam took a corner faster than necessary and Blake had to grab the door handle.

Gage faced forward again. "Liam drives until I say otherwise, got it?"

"Yeah, Gage," Blake muttered.

He let the use of his name not his rank go for now, because Liam was already pulling between two parked black-and-white patrol cars. He parked the giant SWAT van in the center, close to the awning where the scene commander directed everyone. It would be a layer of protection against anyone gawking or cops here.

Gage got out and slammed the door. He strode to Captain McCauley, who he'd trained under at the academy. Liam didn't like him all that much as they'd butted heads, but Gage had always respected the guy. McCauley was over the detectives these days, but they exchanged small talk on occasion.

"What've we got?" Gage slid the helmet on his head and clicked the snap.

McCauley barely looked up. He'd pulled a vest over his suit shirt. "Five guys got out of that van." He pointed toward the curb in front of the bank, where a beat-up van had been haphazardly parked. "And raced in with automatic weapons. Opened fire. Created panic, and then locked down the bank. They're still inside."

Gage frowned. "They left their getaway car out here? How do they plan on getting away?"

"Let's pray they don't just plan to kill everyone inside, and then themselves."

Gage agreed. For years he hadn't prayed much, wasn't raised that way, and didn't like the idea of giving up control. He had things handled.

These days? *Lord, help us. Protect the innocents in that bank.*

"Take your team and get set up. One sniper on the roof of the plaza, the rest of you cover the back exit."

"Copy that." Gage swiped some binoculars off the table and took a look at the front window. "How many hostages?" He needed to get a look at the suspects, so he'd know who to arrest if they ran out the back.

A masked man walked past the window, toward a woman standing up in the center of the lobby.

Dark hair, wearing a business suit. Gage zoomed in on her face, which held not one ounce of fear. "She's in on it." Then he realized who it was. "Clare."

McCauley turned to him. "What did you say?"

SIX

"Woman, you're about to get yourself killed."

Clare stared down the barrel of a gun. "I was thinking the same thing."

She'd only come into the bank to talk with the manager, to offer for Vanguard to go over their security measures in light of a *possible* threat.

Unfortunately it seemed that threat stood in front of her now, very real.

Clare still had on her workday outfit of a skirt suit and heels, no gun. No vest. Certainly not boots, only a helmet and flak jacket. Those were the good old days. Sometimes she thought maybe she preferred life in the army to this civilian existence of nine-to-five and a fluffy pillow. Maybe she'd gone soft.

Instead of talking with the bank manager, a van had screeched to a stop outside and five men raced through the lobby doors into the bank.

"Get over there with the others or I put a bullet in your head." He motioned with the gun.

Instead of blatantly studying him and his friends, she

looked anew at the bank as she backed up to the huddle of patrons sitting on the floor against the cashier counter. Marble floor and walls, columns, colored glass in the windows. Was it supposed to look like a church? She didn't know if that was because this was the altar they worshiped at, or if it was to fool the masses into bringing their alms. She'd had the same thought at the Smithsonian building in Washington, DC, but money instead of science was the religion here.

Clare passed the pile of electronics—phones and smartwatches on the floor. All of it smashed under their bootheels.

They'd sprayed bullets at the ceiling, demanded all hands raised so no one could trip a silent alarm, and locked the doors. Their movements had a level of efficiency to them. They all knew what they were doing, and what their role to play was.

One guy by the door, keeping guard. Two to watch over the hostages, two to head into the vault with the manager and another woman they seemed to have picked out randomly. Clare had done her best to stick out like that. When the other woman was chosen, she'd demanded to take her place. No dice.

All she'd come here to do was recon. Observe and consider that this could be a target at some point. Now she was in the middle of it.

By design?

She didn't believe things happened arbitrarily. Otherwise she would have no hope at all that she could make up for the things she'd done. There would only be despair. Instead, she got the chance every day to work for atonement. To pay back the debts she owed. Had God given her this opportunity to do even more than that.

Was today the day she could give her life for an innocent victim? Finally wipe the slate clean.

The armed man took a couple of running steps, launched off the wall, and zigzagged back to jump up on the island a few feet away.

Clare stopped before she sat and stared.

"Listen up!" He swiped his gun across the gathering of hostages on the ground, glaring. "It won't be long, so sit tight. And if I think anyone is trying anything, I *will* start shooting."

Clare lifted her hands. She wished she could pray, but that wasn't something she'd ever done. And she didn't plan to start now.

The guy to her left stood guard. The one by the door didn't display an ounce of nerves despite the fact the police clearly had the building surrounded.

"You some kind of cop?" He stared down at her from his position standing on the island where she'd signed checks before. "'Cause I don't like cops."

The guy to her left snickered. The first sign of life she'd seen from him, and the guy on the island shushed him pretty quickly. The humor she could see in the mouth slit on his face mask dissipated as it did from his eyes. "One minute."

All five of them had on the same type of clothes. She studied the one on the island, wondering what the minute counted down to.

Their clothes were well-made, high-end all-weather gear. Sweat-wicking, thermal layer to keep you warm—or cool depending on the weather. Clean, new-looking weapons. Brand-label all-black tactical boots she knew were lightweight because she bought them for Vanguard employees. Footwear was something you didn't skimp on.

All five had toned physiques, though she only saw two as they passed initially. These three were built differently, so they weren't genetic relations. Different heights and sizes, but the same toned muscle. Tightly packed but not bulky in a way that would make them heavy and lumbering when they needed to make a quick exit.

"So what's the plan?" They had about thirty seconds by her count. "Because I can help you."

"Not a cop, but what?" He hopped off the island and strode to her.

Clare lifted her hands, not just to ward off his attempt to intimidate her with his proximity. She showed him her pocket and tugged out—slowly—a business card. "Vanguard Investigations."

"Like private eyes?"

"Among other things." It clearly stated her name. He'd be able to find her later, which posed a risk to her personal safety. But she needed to solve this more than she needed to protect herself from harm.

"And you're the CEO?" He looked her up and down. "Fancy."

He didn't want to be bested by a woman. He was young, probably midtwenties. She'd seen more life by then than he had. It wasn't just war that prematurely aged a person. "I can help you negotiate your way out of this. After your friends have retrieved what you came here for, of course."

His lips curled up in a smirk.

"No one needs to get hurt."

A gunshot echoed from the vault, followed by gasps and screams.

Clare and the gunman stared at each other. Neither flinched.

"Let's not drag this out," he said.

"Agreed." She wanted to avoid bloodshed. Or no *more*, at least. She thought through what she knew of the back alley. The sewers. A tunnel maybe, but they hadn't brought backpacks of explosives in with them. In fact, all they had were their weapons and whatever they'd tucked in the pockets of their high-tech tactical pants. They could go up to the roof, then jump to the neighboring building. Or base jump.

Some other plan to get around the cops.

"Got it." The man called out from the vault, behind the cashier's counter. "Let's go."

All three men raced to their friends. They met in the rear of the lobby and raced to a door in the back hall. A formation. Practiced escape, almost choreographed.

Clare reached the open end of the counter when the guy she'd faced off with turned and fired twice in her direction.

She ducked down behind the counter. Glass shattered, and someone screamed.

Wherever they went, she'd be right behind them. However they got away, she would be there to see it. Without a gun she couldn't take them out—or take them down. But if she tracked them down and handed them over to the police, it would secure her company's standing in the law enforcement community in Benson.

Clare ran after the thieves, to the back hall.

Up the stairs.

SEVEN

The young man stared him down. "I'm just saying, Clare Juarez is inside that bank."

McCauley snorted. "So we should all go home?"

Gage's stomach hurt he'd been clenching it so hard. Clare wasn't the girl he'd known in high school. It couldn't be her. He wasn't going to let his mind go there right now. "Plenty of people in that bank, and intel said five assailants." He shifted the grip he had on his weapon, clipped to the front of his vest.

Liam and the guys had deployed around the bank while Gage waited for further orders from McCauley.

Then this guy showed up saying Clare was his boss.

Gage knew all about Vanguard Investigations. He didn't have a problem with them, but that might be because he'd never crossed paths with any of their people. Everyone knew Vanguard hired ex-cops and criminals. If that was how Clare ran her business then it said something of the caliber of person she was, didn't it?

"She can take care of herself," the guy said. "And she'll take care of the people inside."

Gage squared on the guy. "What did you say your name was?" He wasn't even midtwenties. He had training. That was clear just in the way he moved. But the guy was new to this, whereas Gage had been a cop nearly fifteen years.

"Peter Olson."

"And Vanguard sent you as their spokesperson?"

"We monitor the police band and the GPS location of all staff members. Clare pinged as inside the bank."

"I know she's in there." Gage wanted to fold his arms, but the rifle clipped to his front prevented that. He'd seen her through binoculars. Honestly he wouldn't have been surprised if seeing her landed him on his butt. The term *floored* absolutely applied here.

McCauley jogged him out of his thoughts. "You and her have history?"

The Vanguard guy didn't say anything, and Gage wasn't going to answer in front of anyone else. Not that he and McCauley had anything between them but professional respect. "Let's just get those hostages out and get the suspects detained, shall we? This isn't personal."

He walked away then, out from under the awning where McCauley had set up scene command. The last thing he needed was Clare invading his life right now. His history with her was just that—ancient. As the new lieutenant of SWAT he needed a laser focus on his team and the job.

Otherwise he'd lose everything he'd been working toward his entire career. Or since the day he realized Clare had left him to his life and gone on with hers.

The front doors to the bank opened, and people started to run out.

Chaos erupted.

The first few people, dressed in office attire, lifted their hands. Cops yelled for them to get down. No one expected the hostages to flee out the front door, unless something had happened inside.

Gage keyed his radio. "Sit rep on four."

The SWAT team had their own channel, and since the uniforms here could take care of hostages, he had the guys switch to it.

Liam came on first to channel four. "Back doors are shut. No movement."

"I've got something on the roof." Dakota's voice was steady in a way Gage needed right now. The guy might have issues, but he focused like the professional he was when the situation demanded it. Who wasn't a hot mess when they took off the uniform at the end of the day and were left to their own devices?

Gage said, "Go ahead, Masterson."

"Door open on the roof. Five males exited, masks, and one had a backpack. All armed."

Gage headed for the front door, fighting through the crowd to get close to it.

"They're using a zip line on the roof," Dakota added.

Gage stopped. "Which direction?"

"East."

He looked up at the height of the bank. "Tell me where it ends. The rest of you, head for the end on foot. I'll bring the van."

Gage jumped in the driver's seat, not bothering to adjust it from Liam's six-two frame to his five-ten. He just sat on the edge of the seat and flipped on his lights and siren. He made sure people got out of his way as he wound through emergency vehicles headed east.

"A woman exited after them." Dakota paused. "She can't go after them dressed like that." He sounded like he was talking to himself with that last part.

"What's she doing?" Gage didn't want to ask what she looked like so he could confirm it was Clare. They'd realize he knew her, and he'd have to deal with more questions than just the ones from McCauley and whoever had overheard. Word would get out they had history, but that didn't mean anyone would find out the truth.

Two buildings down, he cut through an empty side street.

Better this way, getting away from the scene. He didn't need to run into Clare—not if he could help it. She would be back at the bank and he could do his job. Arrest the bad guys.

Dakota got on and gave him the street name. "Can't see where they landed, but they were about twenty feet off the ground there."

"I'm in pursuit," Liam said. Then he updated the street name, one that ran perpendicular to the one Gage was driving down.

"I'm with the sarge." That was Blake.

"Mast and I will call McCauley, then head your way." Jasper wanted to watch Dakota's back, that was fine by Gage.

He would trust his brother to take care of Dakota and handle whatever happened. The team operated that way, and had since the beginning, because they were friends first. Only now that Gage was in charge it seemed like an uphill battle to try to get them to see him as their boss rather than just their teammate.

"Copy that." Gage spotted Liam and Blake running. He pulled over ahead of them.

A mangled car on the side of the road had been shoved aside partially onto the curb. Liam slowed to a jog, then stopped beside it. Gage jumped out the SWAT van. Liam rounded the car to the passenger side and bent. "Doesn't look like anyone is inside."

"What happened?" Gage stopped beside Blake.

"White box van. No plates." Blake pushed out a breath, then another. Sweat dripped down his forehead. "They zip lined down right beside it, jumped in, and took off within seconds. Hit this car on the way out. Took off."

"Which way?" Gage could get dispatch to check traffic cameras. Put a BOLO out. They also needed evidence technicians to pull paint transfer from the mangled vehicle to see what they could find out about the brand used on the escape van.

Blake took another breath, finally catching it to try to slow his heart rate. His gaze snagged on something behind Gage, but he said nothing. "Fenton, going toward Bannock."

"I'll call it in." Gage peeled back Velcro from his thigh pocket on his cargos and tugged out his cell phone, already turning away.

She stood right behind him.

Dakota's voice came over the radio. "The woman from the roof had the same idea as us."

Gage pressed his lips together. *Now you tell me.*

She was slightly out of breath. A little pink in the cheeks. A woman, where the person he'd known years ago had been a girl. She stood before him now a beautiful woman who was a stranger.

Her eyes flared. "Gage."

Blake spun to her.

Gage didn't need him getting into this. "Clare." He cleared his throat and fought back all the emotion that rose up to choke him alive. "Good to see you."

He stepped past her and made his phone call.

There was work to do.

EIGHT

Clare kept still. He walked away, past her. Dismissing her completely, as though they didn't have more history than Niagara Falls running over their pasts. Their lives would forever be tangled together, whether he liked it or not.

Even if he seemed to want to remain in denial.

Clare glanced over her shoulder, biting her lip between her teeth. Nearly twenty years, and she knew now that connection had never gone anywhere. Gage Deluca held a piece of her. Always had, always would.

No matter that he tore her heart out the first time he walked away. He clearly thought nothing of it—or didn't care at all.

Clare sucked in a long breath through her nose that was supposed to calm her. She shifted her weight and winced. After running in these heels all the way down the block, she wasn't looking forward to walking back to the bank to retrieve her things.

Not to mention up and down the stairs.

If she could've used that zip line to get down here, she would have.

The thieves had escaped in a vehicle.

She turned back to the African American officer behind her. His nameplate said *Reed*. "Did you get a license plate on the getaway vehicle?"

He blinked. "You were inside the van...ma'am?"

"It's Clare. You've heard of Vanguard Investigations?"

"Sure." He nodded. "Who hasn't?"

This guy was the king of not giving anything away. An asset in his job, but not helpful for her trying to gauge how he—and his team—felt about her. "Is Gage Deluca your boss?"

Reed nodded. "You know the lieutenant?"

"A long time ago, I did."

"I see."

She had no idea what he saw. Clare couldn't even begin to guess.

"Ma'am, you'll need to provide a statement to the police since you were in the bank."

"I'll have to walk back to the building." The way Gage seemed to have. Walking off steam? She could do that, but it would hurt. She winced again at the thought of that many steps in these shoes.

"Come on." Reed motioned to the SWAT van. "I'll drive you."

He probably thought she was a flight risk he shouldn't let out of his sight. Still, she really didn't want to walk and had no phone because the thieves had taken it.

His colleague with the sergeant stripes on the shoulders of his bulletproof vest came over. "Reed, you stick here. Keep the scene secure. I'll take her back to the bank."

"Sure, Lee." Reed whirled around, back to the wrecked car.

The sergeant held the front passenger door for her and held one elbow to help her up.

"Thanks." After all, her mother had always taught her to be polite. Even when the reception she got was Juneau frosty.

The minute she sank into the seat it hit her. Cinnamon.

Clare closed her eyes as her mind jumped back to days—and nights—that summer before senior year. Trips to the lake. Camping. A hundred things they shouldn't have done, and all the consequences that came with it.

Heartbreak not the worst among them, but high on the list.

He chewed cinnamon gum still.

Clare didn't want to think about how it hit her that she knew it about him and it'd been true all these years. She'd traveled the world, seen unspeakable things. Witnessed hope and determination firsthand. Started a business. So many other things, and he'd been here all this time. Steadfast. Immovable.

"Clare Juarez." The sergeant gripped the wheel and turned the van in the middle of the street to head back to the bank.

"What's your name, Sergeant?"

"Liam O'Connell."

She didn't want to repeat the question she'd asked Officer Reed, so she kept her mouth closed. The team would stand by their lieutenant, but there was more that was personal between Gage and this Liam guy. He'd be the one Clare would have to win over.

If that was even on the table.

Which it most decidedly was not.

He slowed outside the bank and put the van in park, turning to her about to say something.

"Thanks for the lift." Clare shoved the door open and hopped out before he could. Like the coward she was.

As soon as she closed the door behind her, Peter jogged over. "Clare!"

"Hey, did you just get here?" she asked.

He shook his head. "Were you really inside, boss?"

"I caught them escaping on that zip line. Raced back down the stairs and tried to reach the end, but they'd gone."

Peter frowned. "Blew right past the police cordon. I'm guessing the whole department is after them now." He handed her his tablet. "Write down every detail while it's fresh in your mind."

Clare got started, finding a brick wall in front of the bank so she could sit and type on the tablet with both hands. Once she got going, she found she could recall more details than she knew about the five suspects that might point to who they were. Even the stitching on the shirts. She recounted every-thing from start to finish, ending with the paint transfer on that wrecked car but excluding the fact she personally knew the SWAT commander.

No one she worked with needed to be part of her personal angst. Even if she would rather they treated her like one of them, at least sometimes. In this case, that would mean telling them all the tragic details of her and Gage and what happened.

"Here." She handed Peter the tablet and stood. "Send a copy of that to the police department."

"Because we want them to know everything we know?"

Clare turned back to him. "In this case, that gets the suspects in cuffs faster."

"Except if we pursue them ourselves, without the police looking over our shoulders, we could bring them in ourselves."

"Do you want me to tell your brother-in-law that you cut

out the PD on purpose?" Never mind it was knowingly putting people's lives in danger—or it could.

Peter made a face.

"I didn't think you'd want to tell Lucas that."

"So we're working with the cops?" he asked.

"I didn't say that."

Peter frowned.

"Giving them all the information we have doesn't mean we're working with them. And it doesn't mean we can't find the suspects first and bring them in ourselves." Clare lifted her brows and saw him smile.

"Russ is inside," Peter said. "Wanna tell him that?"

Clare laughed. "We didn't sign a contract. We're just taking a look." She headed for the front doors of the bank. "I'll see you back at the office."

"I'll hang out. Follow you." Peter shrugged. "Just to make everyone feel better."

She liked that they cared, even if it wasn't necessary to cover her. Doing that tended to cost people their lives. Which was why she was the boss—so she didn't have anyone in her line of fire.

Standing out in front meant she took the fire for them. Not the other way around.

A cop stood at the door, which had been propped open. She gave her name and was admitted into the busy room bustling with people. Russ stood in a huddle with Captain McCauley and Lieutenant Deluca—which was how she was going to think about him.

"I just need my personal belongings," she said. "Then I'll get out of your hair."

If Gage didn't want to acknowledge her that was fine. She could be a professional.

"Clare!" Russ Franklin, the Benson PD Commissioner,

strode over, spread his arms, and enveloped her in a hug. "Thank the good Lord you're all right."

She found her face smashed up against the collar of his wool coat. When he leaned back, she said, "There was a gunshot in the vault. Was someone shot?"

"I just watched the surveillance video. You're lucky it wasn't you."

NINE

"What does he mean?" Gage strode toward Clare and his boss's boss. "What did you do?"

Russ Franklin might be over the whole police department, but the boots-on-the-ground guys saw him as a paper pusher. The mayor's attempt to put a known guy in the role, someone the blue-collar guys would respect since he'd been a US marshal before he retired. Gage liked the guy, except Russ just went down in his estimation since he was close with Clare.

Not that Gage planned on making people take sides.

McCauley moved to stand by him, and the captain rocked back and forth on his shoes. "She stood up to one of the suspects. Probably kept a whole lot of hostages safe by keeping them focused on her."

Russ took up where the captain left off. "Unarmed. No vest. You just stand up to three guys with guns like it's no big deal?"

Clare looked at Russ. "You know it's never no big deal."

Russ nodded.

Gage pressed down on his back molars. What was that

about? He couldn't ask or he'd have to admit he knew next to nothing about this woman. He was tempted to take a step to the side and do a web search for her company. Surely there was an "About" page that would list her credentials.

Would that tell him who she was?

He thought she might've been a marshal, where she'd have worked with Russ, but there was something about her manner that didn't say "fugitive taskforce."

He'd been focused on SWAT, no time for socializing. Or, apparently, realizing what was going on in his hometown. How long had she been back?

Forget it. "SWAT needs a copy of that footage. If we're going to identify and locate the suspects." *Focus on the case.*

Otherwise, he'd only end up with her destroying him all over again. Walking away and taking everything he wanted with her. Leaving him with the nothing he'd always had.

With his luck, she'd take his career with her as well and there'd be no way to stop her ruining everything he'd built.

"Lieutenant Deluca is right," Russ said. "The PD will cover this. They'll find these guys before anyone else gets hurt."

Clare's jaw flexed. "You're revoking your offer?"

"It's not like that," the commissioner said. "It's about keeping people safe."

"What happened?" she asked.

Gage figured she was gearing up to argue about whatever Russ's offer had been. "A teller was executed in the vault. Wanna tell us about how you followed the suspects up to the roof where you were going to...what—confront them with your bare hands?"

"It's about gathering intel. That's my job." Her eyes flashed gold, the deep brown flaring with life like they did when she dug her heels in. "I wrote up a report already, and my office will forward it over."

Gage didn't want to work with her. Nor did he want to be impressed with what she'd accomplished just observing. She'd found the car wreck the same as his team had.

"Thanks for your help." He turned to Captain McCauley. "SWAT can handle this case."

Technically, he needed to ask permission to run with it. Instead, he'd slightly demanded it, but McCauley could probably figure out this wasn't a normal situation. He'd pegged it earlier that Gage and Clare had history. He had no idea.

McCauley was African American, while Gage had always assumed he had some of that in him. He had no idea—he was essentially a mutt. His mom never told him who his father was, and if she'd dated he never knew about it. With that many secrets between them, it was no wonder they weren't that close.

He lived his life, and she did the same. They just didn't overlap that much. The cops in the department appreciated there was always someone happy to take their Thanksgiving or Christmas shift who didn't care they were working a holiday.

McCauley said, "Commissioner?"

He didn't answer right away, so Gage turned to look. The older man glanced between Gage and Clare. As if there was something to find by assessing them standing nearly side by side. "Let's give Vanguard a shot to provide resources that would slow down the investigation if SWAT used our traditional routes. How does that sound?"

Clare's face got that pinched look it always got when she was pleased with herself. "Just as long as no one else gets hurt."

"You really didn't know that happened?" Gage wanted to

say more, really rub it in for the brass. Instead, he let it hang there and figured they'd fill in the gaps.

"I'm sure the two of you can figure out all the particulars. Work the case. Figure this out." Commissioner Franklin rocked back and forth on his dress shoes. "Show us what you can do." He turned to McCauley. "Keep me apprised, Captain."

McCauley said, "Yes sir," and followed the boss to the front doors of the bank.

"I'll send you a copy of my report." Clare kept her face blank of any expression. "Just because Vanguard is assisting doesn't mean we need to see each other."

Over her shoulder he spotted the Vanguard guy, Peter Olson, enter. Gage realized this guy had a sister who was an EMT. He'd met Freya before—the responsible, upstanding half of the family.

Gage figured he had to say something. He settled on, "SWAT will let your office know when we need any help. Why don't you give me the number for your lab. Just in case." Then he wouldn't have to contact her at all.

Peter found them in the crowd, turned back, and held the door for someone else—a young woman about the same age as him with the same coloring as the woman in front of him.

"Clare!" the younger one called out as she ran across the lob. "I heard what happened." She slammed into Clare, and they hugged. "Are you okay?"

Clare nodded through the lean back. "I'm fine, Selena."

"Selena, is it?" Gage glanced at Clare. "Is she my daughter?"

The girl was about the right age—the right coloring. Last he'd seen Clare, she'd been pregnant with his child. Then she was just gone. Both of them were gone.

Selena whirled around. "Clare isn't my mom."

So he was wrong about this. "Okay—"

She cut him off. "My mom's name was Kara, and she died in Kunar Province, laying down cover fire for her teammates so they could survive and get out of there, even if that meant they could carry her out. And ship her home in a pine box."

Clare's eyes reddened, filling with tears. "Honey."

Selena shook off Clare's touch. "I'm glad you're okay." She turned and strode to the door, where Peter's expression shot daggers at Gage. Peter followed Selena out of the bank, and Gage realized everyone around them had heard that whole exchange.

"Are you satisfied?" Clare shot him a look.

Gage said nothing, aware his cheeks had heated.

"We were making progress." She lifted her chin. "Thanks for tearing off the bandage and exposing that wound just because you want to be the injured party here."

"And I'm not?" Either way, he didn't have her. Or the life they'd created together.

"We just have to figure out how to work together without actually working together."

"Or you can finally tell the truth about what happened."

"It won't change the past." Clare sniffed. "Let's just be professionals about this." She turned and strode to the door.

Gage stared at her.

Someone slapped his shoulder. "Nice one."

Gage ignored them. *Work together?* This sounded like a great opportunity to bridge that divide Clare carved between them and find out what she was hiding. In fact, he was going to face this in a way that would ensure he got what he wanted. With both barrels loaded and C4 on hand.

SWAT style.

TEN

Clare knocked on the front door. A second later her phone buzzed in her pocket. She flipped her wrist so the notification showed on her watch.

IT'S OPEN.

She let herself into Trey Banning's house, where her friend Ember lived. A couple of months ago, Ember had lost her sister. She received her sister's heart in a transplant and adopted her sister's baby. After Trey put a ring on her finger, he had signed a lease on a studio apartment where he planned to live until the wedding since Ember stayed at his house. Clare got the impression he spent a lot of his off time at the house with Ember and the baby—and he'd even spent some nights on the couch after Trey's mom went back to Last Chance County a couple of weeks ago.

"Hello," Clare called out as she shut the door behind her. She didn't say more, in case it would wake the baby. Laundry covered the living room couch, and a half-drunk cup of tea sat on the coffee table.

Cold.

Clare carried the cup to the sink, where she poured out the rest, discarded the tea bag, and put it in the dishwasher.

"Hey. I just put Cassie down for a nap, so we're good for three minutes or three hours or any amount of time between before she wakes up again." Ember leaned against the doorframe, dark circles under her eyes. It did practically nothing to detract from how gorgeous she was. Seriously, the woman looked like a movie star—something she'd used to her advantage as a CIA agent. Now she wore sweats and a Benson Fire Department sweater that probably belonged to Trey.

Clare smiled at her friend and the normalcy of this whole situation. "Wanna sit?"

"I'll fall asleep." Ember smiled. "Cassie was up half the night. She's teething and crabby, which makes me crabby. Now we're both tired. And super fun to hang around with. I'm pretty sure Trey is going to stay at work as long as possible, and he'll show up later with takeout and flowers."

"I'll help you fold onesies and burp rags," Clare said.

"I won't turn down an offer like that." Ember trailed to the living room.

"How are you doing?" She grabbed the top baby outfit in the pile. She wasn't sure if it was holding baby clothes or talking about Ember's transplant, but Clare's chest ached then. She started a pile of folded laundry.

Ember held a blanket wide, then touched the corners together. "Tired. Apparently that's to be expected and not just my body adjusting to a new heart."

"This is where I crack a joke about you being normal." Clare grinned.

"You and me? Since when."

"We've come a long way since that op in Tangier, that's for sure."

"Eight years. You'd think we would've figured it out by now."

Clare turned and sat on the arm of the couch. "You mean you haven't?" She caught a look at the edge of Ember's expression. "What is it?"

Ember shook her head. "Nope. If I start talking, Trey will hear somehow. Next thing I know he'll drag a preacher over here and marry me in his living room. I want my summer wedding."

Clare smirked. "Okay, bridezilla. You can have a reception in the summer."

"No. It's gonna be special, darn it. I'm not getting married when I'm so exhausted I can barely keep my eyes open at six p.m. Getting married looking all sickly, with a baby on my hip."

"I think probably someone else will hold the baby for you."

"Like you?" Ember fired that shot with no remorse in her expression.

Clare made a face. Her issue with babies had never been noticeable. Now her best friend had a newborn, it was a little harder to steer clear of anything related to pregnancy or bringing a new life into the world.

"I heard about the bank robbery. What were they after?"

"Russ said the bank manager got a hold of the guy whose safety deposit box it was. They took a million in diamonds."

Ember's eyebrows rose. "Which explains why they didn't just grab duffel bags full of cash."

"Diamonds are a whole lot more portable."

Ember nodded.

"And they had to have known that box had that specific item in it." Clare wanted Vanguard to be the ones who figured out who'd told the crew about the diamonds.

"I heard Selena yelled at the SWAT lieutenant."

"How?"

"Trey sent me a bunch of voice messages," Ember said. "He told me the whole story. I think he's still a little gun-shy of Selena, but he knew I'd want to know you got caught up in whatever it was between them."

Clare winced. "He said something that flipped her lid. Actually, I'm pretty proud of her. She faced her grief in a way that didn't suck her back into the hurt."

"What did he say?"

Clare grabbed the next onesie and made folding it far more complicated than it needed to be.

"Uh, spill. *Now.*"

"Did the CIA teach you that interrogation tactic?"

Ember sighed. "Clare."

Her friend was going to be an excellent mom to teenagers when the time came. Not something that would happen for Clare. Ever. Not after everything. Clare shook her head to dispel the cloud of thoughts. "He might've thought she was my daughter." She swallowed. "So he asked if she was also *his* daughter."

Clare grabbed the next item, a blanket, and started folding.

Ember snatched it out of her hand. "I'm sorry, *what*?" She collapsed onto the couch, narrowly missing the folded clothes. Clare moved them to the coffee table. "You...and Gage Deluca? I mean, he's cute and all but..."

"We were seventeen." Clare frowned. "And what do you mean, *but*? But what? What's wrong with Gage?" She slumped into the armchair by the couch and tried to brush off what that question meant.

"Seventeen." There was no judgment in Ember's gaze.

Neither of them had always done the right thing. Ember

was probably the last person in the world who would condemn Clare for a decision she'd made so long ago.

"So did you...give the baby up for adoption?"

Clare swallowed past the lump in her throat. "Gage disappeared after I told him I was pregnant. Both our moms flipped out. He probably couldn't handle it."

Ember frowned.

"He didn't return any of my calls. His mom told me to get lost when I went to their house. I tried a couple more times, but it became clear he wasn't interested in being involved, and my desperation started to wane." Clare felt the burn of tears in her eyes. The only reason she wasn't outright crying was the years between that day and now. "I spent a couple of days in bed, pretty much devastated about the breakup. I had no idea what to do about the baby. My mom dragged me to the cabin. I spent the summer there after..."

"What happened?"

"I miscarried a couple of weeks after I found out I was pregnant." Clare sniffed. "I guess God knew I couldn't handle it. He didn't want me to wreck a baby's life, so he took the baby away. He, or she, is in heaven. Happier than how it would've been with me."

She ran both hands to her knees and stood. "Anyway—"

"Clare—"

"It's ancient history now." She went to the doorway. "Let me know if you need anything, okay? I've got stuff to do."

"You don't need to run from me. Not with this."

Fresh tears pricked her eyes. "I just have to deal with him being part of my life. Until this case is done, and then I can sign a contract with the police department and my people can take care of it from there. I'll go open another branch of Vanguard in Rio, or something."

She headed for the door and let herself out quietly. All

she had to do was guard her heart. Gage stood between her and what she wanted for her company, but Clare didn't plan to let that stop her from getting her employees the contracts that would level them all up.

She would face it all for the chance to make Vanguard a success.

ELEVEN

G age dribbled the basketball twice, then passed.
Liam caught it. "We're really supposed to let
Vanguard come up with all our leads?" He passed
it back.

Gage shrugged, then bounced the ball and made a jump
shot.

Liam let it bounce and caught it.

The work side of things had been pushed to one side of
Gage's mind. Not just because they were waiting for evidence
techs to process the scene—both of them. Detectives were
going through footage, and Gage had no desire to stare at
Clare on screen, over their shoulders.

It was after eleven anyway, and the guys needed to blow
off steam.

"Vanguard can process physical evidence faster than the
department can," he said. "You know we're always on the
lookout for quality third party companies that know what
they're doing to take some of the load running trace
evidence. Not everyone understands how to handle chain of
evidence."

Liam sighed. "I looked her up. Army veteran, local business owner."

Gage frowned.

"I know a guy." Liam shrugged. "There's nothing in Clare's army personnel file about a dependent, so if she had a kid, they don't know. Just a lot of stuff about commendations. Special operations. Words like 'exemplary' and 'fast track.'"

"Great." So what happened to their baby, the one she'd been carrying the last time he'd seen her? Gage scratched at the back of his neck. "Let's just focus on the case, yeah?"

The door at the far end of the gym opened and Jasper walked in, followed by Blake and Dakota. Blake's dark-colored eyes studied Dakota. Gage got a read on how they were doing just by watching them walk.

Jasper was nervous but had the situation under control because he was going to use all the skills his Senator father had taught him. Dakota had closed off, but he was here and that apparently meant they should all be satisfied. Blake, it seemed, spent every minute wondering what would explode next. Not the first time Gage had wondered what was in Blake Reed's past that made him think that way.

Jasper unzipped his sweater and tossed it on his duffel bag. Sneakers squeaked the floor, and Liam bounced the basketball. Jasper lifted his hands. "We gonna do this or not?"

Dakota said, "I'd rather hear about the shouting match Gage got into with a witness at the bank."

Gage accepted the ball from Jasper and turned. "The gal who yelled at me wasn't a witness. She wasn't even there." He bounced the ball a couple of times.

No, not a hostage. Just a young woman he'd thought for a second might be his daughter. The one Clare gave birth to after she broke it off with him. So what happened to his child if that young woman wasn't her? Did Clare have a kid—probably in college by now—and she wasn't planning on letting him into their life?

Exhaustion from the rollercoaster day he'd had settled on him.

Gage bounced the ball and took a shot again. It bounced off the rim. Blake ran in and caught the rebound, scooping it in the basket before his feet hit the ground. The guy could've been a pro ball player, but given the elbows he liked to throw, Gage didn't quite know what to make of Blake.

Out of all of them, he kept his personal life close to the vest. Or hidden under it.

On the outside he was the same color as them—blue. But each one had different upbringings. Jasper's dad was a senator. Gage was raised by a single mom. Blake had a big family because he always had a sister, brother, or cousin calling to ask for a favor. Dakota had a much older brother, Will, who was some kind of federal agent. He'd grown up spending summers with the guy when he could, mostly to escape their father.

Overhead lights glared at him. The guys fell in, and they got the game going. A couple kids from the neighborhood who hung out in the game room when they weren't messing around in the gym and getting into trouble came in the gym. One had a ball, so they probably wanted to play. He was about to ask when they all sat on the bench to watch.

Since there were five of them, not an even six, they settled on what amounted to dog fight basketball. Basically a free for all of every man for himself—with some showing off rolled in.

When Dakota's phone rang for the third time, Gage held on to the ball and turned to him. "You gonna answer that?"

"Why?" Dakota motioned for Gage to throw him the ball. "It's just my brother, Will."

"And you're avoiding him why?"

Dakota shrugged. "The Lord told him I had a need. Something like that means he needs to bug me just to tell me he's *praying for me.*"

Gage had plenty of buddies or knew guys on the force who were Christians. Clare had been one when they dated in high school. To him it just seemed like a bunch of rules, and if it wasn't how he planned to live his life anyway then why change for some arbitrary reason? He liked who he was.

He threw the ball to Blake, who said, "Your brother calls, you should answer."

Dakota shot him a look. "You don't know nothin' about it. Your family is draining you dry, so all you've got is ratty sneakers you're about to walk out of."

Liam was already moving. He got in front of Dakota while Gage spun to Blake. "Don't let him."

Blake could be vicious fighting for a cause he believed in. That cause didn't need to cut Dakota down to size when the guy was already fragile dealing with whatever was going on. Gage was almost certain after that sprained ankle two months ago, Dakota had been on pain meds that might be the issue now. Trying to get off them. Battling recurring pain. Freaking out that his SWAT career was over if he couldn't beat the injury.

Gage said, "Let it go for now. Just play."

Blake lifted his hands. He took the ball from Gage and ran down the court, bouncing it as he went. At the last second he jumped and dunked the ball in the basket. The teenage spectators whooped and hollered. Three of them ran over to join the game with Blake.

Jasper had gone to his bag to take a call of his own. Probably from a woman.

Liam still stood in front of Dakota. "You've got problems? Fine. But you don't cut down your teammate. You think he's gonna take a bullet for you when you treat him like trash?"

Dakota's face reddened almost the color of his hair. "I don't need anyone taking a bullet for me." He slapped his chest. "I got it."

"That's what you think?"

Gage agreed with Liam. No way did Dakota have anything but a whole lot of denial about whatever his brother seemed to think needed the Lord's intervention.

"Point, and I'll shoot." Dakota strode past Liam and headed for Blake and the kids, a couple of whom were intent on doing tricks instead of playing the game.

Liam said, "Working this bank robbery case will be good for us. Even if we did get schooled today."

Gage didn't consider the fact the suspects were in the wind that way, but cases weren't a matter of success or failure. They were either open or closed.

Keeping his job, making this teamwork? That was his focus. And it was win or lose, but no way would Gage risk that loss. If it meant working with Clare, then so be it.

Dakota threw the ball. It slammed Gage in the chest, but he caught it.

One of the kids called out, "We gonna play ball, or what?"

Gage grinned. "Let's do this."

TWELVE

L ondon came awake swinging. Two sets of hands, one sat either side of him in the van, held him in the middle seat. Rio and Phoenix. "What..." His voice came out muffled, a strip of tape over the bottom half of his face.

His abdomen thrummed with pain. London inhaled, and shards sliced through his ribs. Broken, or just cracked. Didn't matter. Either way he was in the doghouse—or worse.

Berlin sat in the front seat while Miami drove. Berlin twisted in the chair and looked at him. "Didn't figure you'd wake up before we got there, but it is what it is."

London recalled the savage beating they'd given him before he blacked out. Mostly Phoenix. The guy had a metric ton of rage in him, and it wasn't the first time they'd let him pummel someone bloody.

Usually it wasn't one of their group on the receiving end.

"What did I do?" The words were nothing but a muffled yell behind the tape.

Phoenix snorted.

Rio reached over and ripped off the tape. Miami took a

corner too hard. London knew where they were going, and the knowledge of it settled in him like cold food in his stomach. Made him want to hurl. *You're a dead man.*

"What?" London had to take a breath. "What did I do?"

Berlin's face bore an emotionless expression. "None of us steps out of line. We agreed to that when we started this, and it's worked. We don't deviate from the plan."

They'd jumped him before. Would they explain now? *What did I do?*

"Awfully chatty with that lady in the bank."

"She wasn't a cop. She runs a PI firm. And I didn't tell her anything." London pulled against the ties securing his wrists together. The boys knew what they were doing. He wasn't going to be able to break out of these—even fracturing a thumb wouldn't help. His breath came faster until spots pricked at the edges of his vision.

"We don't deviate from the plan."

London squeezed his eyes shut. He shook against the seat as pain roiled through his body in waves. *Kill me now. Just put me out of my misery.* "You just decided you don't want to split this five ways. Four is a bigger payday. Is that it?"

"Watch your mouth." Miami took another corner.

London was right—they were headed to the lookout. The van had to be dumped. It was a liability now and couldn't be used. They had to dispose of it in a way that meant it couldn't be traced back to them.

He looked at Berlin. "You gonna take us out, one by one. So you keep everything." He twisted to Phoenix. "Or you. Is this your idea?"

Phoenix just smirked and kept staring out the window.

Miami pulled over, left the van in neutral, and didn't put on the parking brake. The four of them got out, exchanging their body heat for the chill of night air. The dash clock read 01:13.

London stayed where he was, tears rolling down his face now.

The van started to move forward with the easy speed of being pushed. Their speed picked up, down the incline.

Until it sailed over the edge.

THIRTEEN

Clare juggled two grocery bags of delivery cartons and a rectangular box of baked goods through the door to what the sergeant on the front desk called "the cave."

"Knock, knock. Can I come in?"

She had the odd urge to call out that there was a woman on the floor. As though this were some kind of single gender residence, not a police department. Maybe it was the smell of old coffee and stale pizza. Minus the beer it could be a college dorm.

"Hello?"

A young, uniformed SWAT officer stuck his head out of what looked like a kitchen over to the right. To the left was a vast room full of desks and file cabinets. Another room seemed to be a small gym. Between the doors the expanse of the room had a huge table, multiple screens on the walls—one of which displayed cable news with the volume down and terrible subtitles ticking away. Supplies had been piled in one corner along with boxes. Cabinets padlocked. More than one gun safe. And one of those boxing mannequins.

"Where should I put this?"

The young man set his coffee down and headed for her. "Why does that smell so good?"

More people came out of the room with desks, three guys and Gage. So five total. She hadn't seen them all outside the bank. "I heard you guys had an early callout." Clare handed over the box. "So I brought breakfast."

The young officer took the box into the kitchen area.

Gage's African American colleague took the bags with a grin. "Cool of you."

Clare nodded. It wasn't exactly a *thanks*, so she didn't say, *You're welcome.*

The blond sergeant and a guy with a fancy watch headed after him, leaving her alone with Gage.

She had to start somewhere, so she said, "Rough call?"

All of them did look a bit rumpled, like they'd rolled in dirt or dust. One of the guys had a bruise on his cheek, but none seemed injured.

"Because you care about my team?" Gage scoffed.

Clare pressed her lips together.

Someone yelled from the kitchen, "Gage, there's a maple bacon bar!"

He strode over, and she followed him to the door, where one of the guys slapped the blond's hand. "No, that's Gage's. Pick another one." He handed Gage the maple bacon donut.

"There are eggs, bacon, and hashbrowns in two containers. The other two are biscuits and gravy, and one is pancakes." Clare shrugged. "I didn't know what you guys liked." But she had called Captain McCauley after Peter told her the SWAT team had gone out on a call at four this morning. He'd given her a solid list on what to order, and she'd worked from there. "You've all been up most of the night, right?"

The blond grinned. "Which means we're all gonna be in food comas in about thirty minutes." He wiped off his hands, a smudge of donut powder at the corner of his mouth, and stuck his hand out. "Sergeant Liam O'Connell."

"Clare Juarez."

The black guy said, "Blake Reed."

Fancy watch guy lifted his chin. "Jasper Hollingsworth." He pointed at the last man, the redhead, who had a mouthful of biscuits and gravy, the container at his chin. "That's Dakota Masterson."

She smiled. "Nice to meet you all."

"Got an update on the case?" Gage asked.

"Here." Before she could answer, the sergeant handed her a full mug of coffee. "Cream or sugar?"

She took it, careful not to spill like the total dork she could occasionally be. "This is good. Thanks."

"Let's go over what you've got." Gage tossed his napkin and walked out of the room.

Clare followed, slipping the flash drive out of her pocket. "Can I plug this in?"

He frowned, now beside the table. She realized it was one of those huge computers the twins loved. Peter and Simon were obsessed with gadgets, and she had to routinely deny their equipment requests when they said, *Because it looks fun* in the reason they needed it column.

"Plug it into the PD system?" Gage stared at her. "So your people can hack the department network? I don't think so."

"You think I'd do something like that?"

"I don't know anything about what you might do."

Clare held her tongue. She could be a professional, civil enough they got along for the duration of this case. She could suck up all her feelings about Gage and the way he'd dropped her like a hot potato. Do the job. "Then maybe you have an air-gapped computer. If you're worried about a security breach."

"Sarge!" He yelled so loud she started, then his eyes narrowed.

Liam appeared at the door. "Yeah?"

"Get me the alligator."

The sergeant headed for the office to grab a laptop while Gage said, "Does that flash drive have what you found on it?"

Clare might as well tell him. "Despite listening to four thousand audio samples over the weekend, I didn't manage to identify the suspect."

Liam snorted. "Must've been fun." He powered up the laptop.

Gage dragged it over to in front of him on the table. "Thanks." His tone very clearly said, *You're dismissed.*

Liam flicked his smirk over to Gage and said, "Coffee?"

"No thanks." Gage didn't look up from the screen. He held his hand out, and she put the flash drive in it. "The bank surveillance has no audio, and no one recorded what happened inside. So we only have your word for it on what the suspect said to you."

"Then you have everything you need, because I recounted it word for word." She sipped her coffee and tried to rein in the need to defend herself. She had no idea why he'd broken up with her. He didn't know what'd happened to their baby, and she did need to tell him. But the reality seemed clear. He'd never cared about her. He just got what he wanted and ended it when she betrayed him by getting pregnant. Like that meant she was diseased.

"Great. We'll work with this today and see what we can come up with."

"I'll let you know if Vanguard comes up with anything on the clothing." They'd have to not only track down where it was purchased but get credit card records and work through the transactions until they were sure who bought the clothes those men had been wearing. "Because the paint from the van is so generic, there's no way to narrow it down. Same with the tire tread they left on the road when they peeled out."

"What about DNA?"

"We're processing it, but there are over three hundred samples so it'll take time." They would be markedly faster than the local lab the PD used, which was generally backed up three weeks.

Clare finished her coffee. "I'm going to grab a refill." Mostly just because she needed a break from him. The way he was would help her be professional, but the hurt she had buried so long ago seemed to want to leak out anyway.

She poured from the carafe and blew out a long breath where no one could see her take a moment.

"You want any of this food?"

Clare turned to find the fancy watch guy—Jasper Hollingsworth—behind her. She was pretty sure he was related to Senator Hollingsworth, but she'd only seen the guy on TV. "I had a smoothie earlier, but I might snag a pastry closer to lunch." She leaned against the counter. "So what's it like working with Gage?"

Two of the guys kept eating. Jasper glanced at the sergeant, Liam, and said, "He's the best lieutenant we've ever had." The others grunted in agreement.

Dakota said, "Did you know he's the one who found that missing girl the other day?"

"No kidding." She took a sip and tried to figure out how she felt about a guy with so much ire being a hero.

Liam said, "Saved her and took down the kidnapper singlehandedly."

"Wow." Another sip.

It was more than hard to reconcile the man she had met the last few days with the boy she'd known. The love of her life—if that was ever true in high school. Didn't matter. He'd shut her out of his life and did the same thing now showing her one side of him, not the hero or good guy his friends thought he was.

She only needed to get Vanguard up and running on its own. Prove she could atone for the past.

She had work, and that was enough.

Because there would never be anything else. God had spoken loud and clear that it wasn't in the cards for her.

Not ever.

FOURTEEN

"This was a terrible idea."

Clare turned back, her strong fingers holding the door. "What was that?"

Gage shook his head. "Nothing. Go ahead."

"Oh, okay." She went first into an open lobby, chrome and white. A clean reception desk at the far end and a door on the right. The chairs weren't meant to be lingered on. Stylish and uncomfortable. He preferred the ratty old couch in the cave.

"It's a bit different from the basement at the police department."

"The setup you guys have is awesome." She shot him a nervous smile. "Though I'm surprised you didn't have one of those little basketball hoops suckered to the wall—or a window."

"It's in the office behind the door, so it's out of sight."

She grinned.

"Ms. Juarez. I wasn't expecting you back so soon." The receptionist sat up straighter in her chair. "And you have a visitor?"

"Sandy, this is Lieutenant Gage Deluca from the SWAT team at Benson PD." Clare motioned to him, trying not to act like a middle school girl bringing the boy she liked home. "He needs a colleague's pass, please."

Sandy stood. "Of course. Right away."

The receptionist moved efficiently, handing him a tablet to fill out his information and sign his name. She used a webcam to take his photo, a pad to record his fingerprints, and handed him a laminated pass. "Keep this with you at all times in the building."

It connected to a clip, so he attached it to his breast pocket, right below the nameplate on his uniform. "Thank you."

Sandy blushed.

"This way." Clare strode to the door on the right, slid back a panel by the door, and scanned her hand. The light above the door turned green. "You're good walking up the stairs, right?"

Gage didn't know why the smile had gone. Probably for the best, since he needed to keep his guard up being in her sanctuary. She had built this life for herself—without him in it. "Stairs are fine."

"Thanks for taking the time out of you day to come here."

He'd brought his radio and his own car, so it wasn't a hardship to be close to town and available to run at a moment's notice if a call came in. "We're going to be working together. Might as well see what you guys have got."

She nodded and they climbed four flights of stairs, which didn't wind either of them. Clare hadn't left the army because of an injury or anything else that might've happened to her physically.

"How many employees?"

"Fifteen so far." She did the handprint thing again and opened the next door into an office space with cubicles. "We're interviewing for another open spot in cold cases, trying to grow that department. And I've heard wind of a rash of kidnap and ransom incidents in South America lately. So I'm talking with a few former colleagues about expanding our K&R department so we can take more of those kinds of jobs." She shrugged. "Who knows what the future will hold? I just want to build a business that can benefit not just this community, but the world."

"It's impressive."

She shrugged. "I do what I can. What I feel like I need to."

Gage wasn't sure why she'd feel the need to save the world. If there'd been anything in her army file he needed to know about, Liam would've told him. The question was whether Clare would tell him herself.

She hadn't told him what happened with the baby.

After all this time, he'd been through so many cycles of believing one thing, or another. He didn't know what to think now. Except that he'd gone back and asked Captain McCauley if there was another way of doing this, aside from working with Vanguard. He'd been shot down. Gage liked his job. He wanted to keep his job. Therefore, he had to tread carefully.

He hadn't been lieutenant over SWAT long. He still had to prove himself.

Now that Clare had inserted herself into his case, he was between a rock and a hard place.

Make the most of it.

He looked around, oddly curious in a self-destructive way. He didn't need to know that she'd done so well for herself. He had a good life and was at a great place in his career.

Gage spotted Peter from the bank...except this version was skinnier. His twin? Detective Lucas Westbrook had said his fiancée had twin brothers. He lifted his chin. The guy sat back down. Most of the desks were occupied, but it was Monday morning.

"This way." Clare led him down the hall. "We can talk in my office."

The hall had carpet. Artwork on the walls looked good, not just generic hotel art most places decorated in.

Her office was different. Even the receptionist looked a little more put together than the rest of them. It made him want to introduce her to Jasper. The two of them could go out for fifty-dollar steaks, and she'd eat three bites and claim she was full.

He'd rather go to a ball game and get a hot dog.

By himself.

Clare held the door again. He stepped into her office, and the noise level dropped right away. Sound proofing. One wall had a set of windows. He walked over and touched the glass. "Bulletproof?"

"Reinforced, at least. Not much is bulletproof these days."

"What other fancy stuff do you need to show me?"

Clare blinked. "That's not..." She let out a breath through pursed lips. "Can we talk?"

"Sure." He folded his arms. "Why the army?"

She turned away, and he was sure she would refuse to answer the question until she went to a credenza and opened the doors. He moved to stand behind her and looked over her shoulder. One folded flag. "My best friend, Selena's mother." Beside the flag was an array of framed photos. It was hard to recognize Clare in full fatigues, but he did.

"You joined young."

"Right out of high school." She turned to him then. "It

was the furthest thing from what my mom wanted me to do." A ghost of a smile washed over her face. "She still can't believe I did it."

"She's still getting on your case?"

Clare shrugged one shoulder. "She lives in Seattle. Still a top dollar cutthroat lawyer. How about you? How's your mom?"

Gage paused. "She passed away a couple of months ago."

"Oh no." To her credit, she seemed genuinely sorry for him.

"We weren't that close." He wanted to shrug but found that he couldn't.

"Your mom was always nice to me."

Maybe she remembered wrong. "She wasn't nice behind your back." He probably shouldn't speak ill of the dead, but he'd rather be realistic than a liar or someone who remembered things with rose-colored glasses.

His mom had told him it was best to be rid of Clare. They'd tried looking for her, but his mom didn't put much effort into it. He'd tried to file a missing person report, and the detective laughed at him. A younger cop in uniform pulled him aside, got him a cup of awful coffee, and let Gage unload the whole story.

That cop had been killed in the line of duty a couple of years later, but the impression he'd left on Gage would last forever.

"Can we maybe"—Clare bit her lip—"go out for dinner later? Talk about everything."

"Why don't you just tell me if you had an abortion. Or did you give our baby up for adoption?"

A tear spilled from the corner of her eye. She started to speak, but his radio squawked.

He listened for a second.

"What is it?" Clare sniffed and cleared her throat.

"A van was found in the ravine."

"Our van?"

He nodded. "There's a body inside."

FIFTEEN

"Y ou keep a change of shoes in your car?"

Clare looked up from tying her hiking boot, sat on the edge of her trunk with the door open overhead. Gage looked past her, into her little SUV. They'd driven to the trailhead separately, which gave her time to figure out how to tell him she'd lost the baby. But *lost* sounded like missing, so she hadn't settled on a good way to say it yet.

Now the moment was gone, and this wasn't the time or place to get into their personal thing.

"Shoes," Clare said. "Two blankets, a shock blanket, a full medical kit. MREs. A case of waters. Two sets of clothes and winter gear. And an umbrella." Along with her phone, she also had a gun tucked under her jacked in a holster at the small of her back. Just in case.

"And a shovel?" He blinked.

She twisted and picked it up from beside the plastic tote bin. "The kind that folds up."

"Huh." He stared as though he didn't know what to make of her.

That went both ways. Lieutenant Gage Deluca was

nothing like teenage Gage. She had grieved a moment for his mother on the way over, even with what he'd said about her. The idea his mom had talked badly about Clare behind her back wasn't entirely surprising. She'd done that about people she met, disparaging perfect strangers she'd seen at the grocery store in a way that seemed mean and sometimes prejudiced.

But she'd loved her son. Not in an over-the-top, touchy-feely way, but Clare had seen it in her.

She set her boot down. "I'm ready."

Clare hit a button inside the tailgate door, and it beeped and started to close. Then she slid her sunglasses to the top of her head, since the cloud cover was back. When the sun broke for three minutes through the clouds, the day was bright enough she needed them. After that, it was back to clouds.

They headed for the trail, giving their information to the officer with his clipboard. Smoke hung in the air, but there were no fires nearby. A fire department vehicle had been parked a few spaces down from where she left her vehicle, so she figured the situation was handled.

Gage still wore his uniform. The officer called him "sir." Clare had been the recipient of that respect in the military, with her officer rank. Now she no longer held it, the respect was different. Her employees treated her similarly, but if she was honest, she'd rather go back to the camaraderie of teammates.

Even with all the employees and the close relationship she now had with Ember, Clare had to admit it was lonely living by herself.

Not enough to entice her into a relationship. Just enough she noticed it, and then had to force herself to ignore the longing in her.

"Whoa."

Gage's exclamation jogged her from her thoughts. Clare looked around and saw what he'd noticed. "Oh. Wow."

The van lay upside down, completely burned out but no longer on fire. Two uniformed firefighters with radios over one shoulder hung back, observing. Chatting with each other and drinking from hot cups.

Clare spotted a woman she knew—the medical examiner, Sarah Carlton. Though she was married now, Sarah had kept her name in a professional capacity. Her husband was a quiet person Clare had met once and quickly afterward signed a nondisclosure agreement with some mutual friends.

Sarah stood out of her crouch by the window. She took a heavy breath, her face pale. "Ohhh." She strode to the tree line and put one gloved hand against a trunk. She leaned forward and made some moaning noises.

Clare strode over. "Hey, you okay?"

Sarah pursed her lips and blew out a breath. Gage showed up beside Clare and held out a water bottle. "Here."

She drank some slow sips. "Most of the time I'm fine. Then it hits me. But *do not* tell Joseph. If he asks, I was completely fine."

Clare frowned and glanced at Gage, unsure how much he knew about Sarah and her husband and his history. His life had been lived at terminal velocity for so many years there had been a path of destruction. Now they finally had the chance to be happy and live their lives in peace. "Don't you think he'd want to know if you're unwell?"

"Only if I actually throw up." Sarah took another sip of water. "And who has time for that? I've got a body to get back to the morgue."

"I'm going to go take a look." Gage wandered to the van.

"Okay, *what* is going on between you?" Sarah stepped

closer, her voice barely above a whisper. "Because I'm getting vibes."

Clare wasn't going there. "Are you sure you're okay?"

Sarah glanced at the firefighters, Gage, and a local sheriff's deputy who'd shown up. Then she leaned in. "It's morning sickness."

"Oh. Wow. That's awesome."

"Noteworthy for us, and healing for Joseph. Though, I'm not sure he'll ever get past the fear. It's just part of being a parent. But losing his wife and baby the way he did? Until he holds his children in his arms, something will be on edge."

"Children?"

Sarah grinned. "It's twins."

Something in Clare relaxed. "Twins. That's amazing." She gave her friend a hug because it was wonderful. Knowing it was different from what Clare experienced honestly made it easier. As though she could move the knowledge to a different category. One not so emotionally charged.

Sarah eyed her. "Now spill. You, and Lieutenant Deluca?"

"We're working together on this case. Anything else is ancient history."

"Mmm."

"What's that supposed to mean?" Clare set her hands on her hips.

"Nothing. I should get back to work as well." Sarah took a step back. "My door's always open if you want to chat. Ember and I are talking about starting a book club. You're welcome to join."

"Oh, well." Clare sighed. "I might like to join that." She loved to read and needed to make more time to do it. With the business she'd slacked off the last few years. Convinced herself she was too busy for frivolous things.

"Come on. I'll walk you through what I found so far." Sarah's color had returned. Instead of her skin and lips being the same color, she had pink in her again.

"I remember those days."

"Huh?" Sarah stopped.

"Being nauseous, and nothing got rid of it. But we take the bad with the good." She had been waiting for some good a long time. When Ember came back to town it seemed things were looking up. Now the bad had resurfaced and she had to face the worst of her past with Gage. He needed to know, so she had no choice and wasn't going to complain. The truth needed to be spoken.

But it couldn't be denied the moment she had something good, it was taken away. Or overwhelmed with bad.

Almost like God denied her happiness. Maybe He really did hate her no matter how hard she tried, or the work she did to make amends. She wanted to do the right thing. Why didn't it work?

Sarah touched her shoulder. "You're talking about being pregnant?"

Clare shook her head. "It was a long time ago. It doesn't matter now." She squared her shoulders. "Why don't you show us what you found?"

Her phone buzzed in her pocket, but she ignored it. Whatever it was could wait until this was done, then she'd hopefully have a good excuse to leave.

SIXTEEN

G age felt a drip of rain on the back of his neck. "Guess you needed that umbrella." He shifted so Sarah could see in the van, preferring to look at Clare rather than a burned victim. Not that it was much of a decision.

Clare gave him a flat smile. "What does it look like in there?"

"Not good. It's the van they escaped in, but that will have to be officially confirmed." All of which would go in the report. "Since we saw it, no surprise they dumped it. Given this is the third or fourth place they hit, there's a systematic nature to what they're doing."

Sarah headed for her case and came back with some evidence bags and a zippered pouch.

Clare nodded. "Pushing it off a cliff is one thing." She motioned to the hill and the trees, rutted from the van's rapid descent. A couple of trees had been knocked down, and the van landed a foot into the dirt. "A man inside is another."

Her movements were jerky. Her expression flat.

Gage frowned. Was she okay?

"They've escalated from armed robbery," he said. That meant they'd be even more on edge, determined not to let the police capture them. In fact, they may have gone so far as to commit murder. "If we can ID him that should help us figure this out." At least, he hoped so.

"It will be difficult to get DNA from a body burned this badly." Sarah wiggled back out of the van and stood. "Though, not impossible. I won't rule out the chance we'll get an ID."

Gage relished the chance to push aside all the personal stuff between him and Clare. Maybe she needed that as well. Both of them knew how to focus on the job. He wanted to get back to their conversation, with dinner probably like she'd suggested. But who wanted to have a hard conversation while they were trying to eat?

He didn't know what to do with all the feelings swirling in him, so he prayed. God was supposed to take those things and give him peace. The Spirit of God brought fruit like that, giving Gage yet more things to be thankful for.

"Vanguard would like to take the lead on that."

Gage turned to Clare. "You want that responsibility?"

She lifted her chin. "We can do this. We're professional, and we have the equipment we need. If Doctor Carlton can provide us with the physical evidence, we can run the tests. Focus on identification and anything else that might give us facts concerning this man."

"I doubt he's a victim, though it's possible." Gage just had his gut instinct. He wanted to know what Vanguard would find. "More likely he's one of the suspects."

"So they killed one of their own?" Clare's eyes widened. "Whether by accident or on purpose, they're a man down."

"His hands were bound, so I'm not thinking this was accidental," Sarah said. "It's highly likely they killed him on purpose. For whatever reason."

"Tied up. Pushed over." Gage nodded. "They wanted rid of him. They did it out here, hoping the crash destroyed as much evidence as possible. Means he was a liability, or he crossed them somehow."

There wasn't a good way to determine whether he was the man who'd faced off with Clare in the bank. Maybe they would never know for certain. He wasn't meant to have answers to some things in life before he was in heaven. At least with Clare he had a shot at finding out the truth. He'd waited this long. If it was another day or so, it wouldn't make much difference.

Especially if whatever she had on her phone meant she was about to leave. For some reason he got that read from her body language. Then she took a step back. "I need to go meet someone if that's all right."

Sarah said, "I can have the physical evidence delivered to Vanguard."

"Or I can send a team to collect it," he said. "Either way."

Sarah nodded. "His cheekbone looks swollen, but the burns make it nearly impossible to tell if it's an injury or fire damage to his tissue and skin. I'll let you both know later."

"Thanks, Doc." Gage decided to walk Clare back to the parking lot, but when he turned to go after her, she was already ten feet in front. That meant running to catch up and looking like a loser who had to chase a woman.

Gage didn't have a problem pursuing a relationship, but no one needed to think that was what was happening between him and Clare. All they had was a painful history. Even if he desperately wanted an answer to his question, Gage didn't want it in a parking lot right before she drove off.

He climbed in his car and radioed in that he was taking

lunch. After that he'd head back to the office. Gage grabbed a burger from a nearby drive-through. Close to his mom's house in Benson. Her key was on his keyring, so he headed there and ate his burger in the car on her drive.

When he was done procrastinating, he headed inside. Seeing Clare again had brought up too many memories. He was going to have to clean this place out soon. But talking about his mom with Clare made him wonder if anything in her stuff would give him a clue what he faced.

His mom had rented one unit of a fourplex, and over the years of living there, she had accumulated enough belongings he'd have to get help to haul it all out. Her couch was nicer than his but the wrong color.

And not what he was here for, even if his mind wanted to ignore the feelings and dispassionately catalog things.

He leaned against the entryway wall and stared at the living room and kitchen area. Her tiny round table and single chair gave him the idea she didn't entertain much—or only sat alone at the table. He'd come here a couple of times since she moved in, once when he'd driven her home after she was released from the hospital the first time her heart gave out. She'd dumped her bag and told him to get lost.

Invading her space felt like an act of defiance, even if she was no longer here. As if he would always struggle against who she'd been.

His heart was supposed to be full of God's love now so that he could offer forgiveness to anyone who needed it. His mom didn't need to receive it, wherever she was now. Gage still needed to offer it—for his own sake.

He moved through the house, but it seemed far too weird to be in his mom's bedroom. Gage settled in the recliner in the spare room where she'd put a bookshelf with books and file boxes. Beside the chair she'd left a library book with a bookmark inserted halfway. A novel she'd never finished—that was probably late now. He'd need to return it.

Beyond the book on the tiny table, a file box labeled GAGE had been stacked with photo albums.

He slid it out. Rather than discovering secrets about his mother, would he discover ones about himself? His mom had kept plenty to herself, choosing to complain about ways she'd been slighted or other people's successes and how unfair life was.

The top was a stack of photos—baseball and basketball team pictures. In the fall he'd played football before he decided basketball was better. Patches from track. A couple of race medals. Medical records, invoices for his broken arm in eighth grade. Gage leafed through the papers going further and further back.

He didn't bother reading the report cards. Or his shot record, though that would've been handy to have in his own files.

At the bottom was a manila envelope. Inside was a copy of his birth certificate—and it didn't look like the version he'd seen. This one listed two middle names and his father's name.

Gage Winchester Kyrill Deluca.

"That's my name?" He'd never even heard it before.

The papers he had—his birth certificate and shot record— listed no middle names, which he'd always thought was odd considering that was more common in Europe than the US. His mom always refused to talk about it, like she had better things to do than be his family.

"What on earth?" He stared at the father's name, and everything he'd ever believed spun on its axis, leaving him reeling. "Alistair McCauley."

SEVENTEEN

Clare pulled into a parking space at the empty corner of the lot. From here she could walk over the berm and cross the street easily to get to the park where Selena wanted to meet. For some reason, her boyfriend, Alex, needed to talk to Clare.

They'd gone to Vanguard first, according to her receptionist, Sandy. Clare had asked them to come here.

Leaving the crime scene had been the best thing for her. No way could she have actually looked inside at the burned corpse, formerly someone's family member. A brother. A son. Eventually, Sarah or Gage would have realized.

No one needed to know the issues she had from her time in the army, and for the most part they lay dormant. She knew what her limits were. Even being around that smoke smell had gotten to her after a while, when she'd no longer been able to push it from her mind.

The fact she was going out to see Selena helped a little, except that the young woman looked so much like her mother. At first glance, seeing the two of them at a picnic bench, it could almost have been Kara there with a man.

Clare used the strong, rapid stride to focus her mind and push off all the emotion of being around Gage.

Selena wore the same brand of jeans as the day before, but today they were black. She had a jacket and ball cap, and the hood of her jacket was pulled over the hat.

In similar fashion, Alex had pulled his hoodie up over his head and the beanie that covered his hair. He wore athletic pants and sneakers.

Both of them were in their early twenties. Gage had been right that Selena was the correct age for their child. It wasn't lost on her that their baby would have been Selena's peer. Clare tried not to think about that either as she made her way to them.

"Hey."

Selena started, glancing up from her phone. "Hey."

Alex twisted to look at her. Clare had never met the guy before, though she'd seen pictures and checked him out online. Both Selena and Alex were recognizable YouTubers with huge followings. Clare didn't have that app and rarely watched videos online, even though Selena sent her links all the time with emojis that Clare supposed should have explained what she needed to know.

She stuck out her hand. "I'm Clare Juarez."

He held it for a second. "Alex."

Clare sat across from them, sideways at the bench so she didn't have to swing her legs in and out. Getting caught somewhere unawares was never a good plan, nor was sitting so it took an extra few seconds to get moving. "You wanted to see me?" She needed to be working the case, but if this was important to Selena, then it would help her feel like she was doing good in the girl's life.

Alex looked at the surface of the picnic table for a second, then glanced aside at Selena. "You're sure?"

She squeezed his forearm. "Absolutely."

He looked at Clare. "You're not a cop?"

She shook her head. "No. And I never have been."

"If I confess a crime to you, are you obligated to tell the cops what you know?"

Now there was a telling question. Clare needed to be truthful, but she also wanted him to tell her what he had to say rather than shutting down. "There are ways to play something like that. Ways that work out best for everyone involved and not just the police and their ability to close the case. We have to take people's lives into account, and their freedom."

If he'd done something, he would need to face justice. She wasn't about to help him get away with committing a crime.

For good measure, she added, "Everyone deserves to be treated fairly."

Alex stared at her for a second, then nodded. "Okay." He took a second. "The group of guys who robbed that bank? I know who they are because I'm one of them."

She hadn't recognized his voice, which meant he wasn't the one she had spoken to.

Without her asking, he said, "I was in the vault. I can tell you what happened when that teller was shot."

Clare nodded. "Okay. Why are you telling me this now?"

Selena clung to Alex's arm. "He's in danger. If they find out he talked, they will kill him like they killed the other guy. But he stopped, and there's nothing he can do."

She appreciated everything Selena had just said, but she also needed to hear it from Alex.

He continued, "I didn't know they were going to kill him. Selena's right. I can't get out."

Clare needed as much information as she could get from him before they decided how to move forward. "How did you hook up with them in the first place?"

"Online, mostly. I never met any of them before, but we followed each other and started chatting in DMs."

An electronic record meant that Vanguard could pull the history of those conversations, give or take which app they used. Even an app that was historically untraceable could be accessed if Alex gave them permission to use his account.

"Can you ID them all?" She figured he had at least seen their faces, unless they wore those ski masks every time they saw each other.

He nodded. "I know their tags, not their real names. But I can point out their faces if you have pictures. We all deleted our other accounts after we teamed up, so there's no way to connect us online."

Clare needed to ask the hard question. "Would you be willing to go back in wearing a wire? It's not an actual wire these days, and they use Bluetooth. Get a recording of them talking specifically about what you have all done. Maybe specifically from the person who is the mastermind." She'd be shocked if there was not one clear leader from the group.

Selena gasped. "He could get killed if they find out he's informing on them to the police."

Clare wondered if that was all this was. "It's the first thing the cops are going to ask Alex if he's willing to do." She paused for a second. "Were you there when the van went over?"

He nodded, and she got a vibe from his expression.

"Did you help push?"

Another nod.

"Participating will get you in trouble. The police will have the leverage they need to get you to cooperate because you'll be convinced it'll keep you from jail. However, it's all about the deal you can make with the district attorney." She tapped her finger on the top of the picnic table. "You need a great lawyer in your corner."

Alex sniffed. "I didn't think he'd actually do it. Then all of a sudden the van was going over the edge. I couldn't do anything to stop it."

"We're going to figure this out." She glanced between them. "You did the right thing, bringing this to me. Because if the police find you first, then you're painted forever as one of them. Coming forward sets you apart as willing to do the right thing." Clare stood up. The two of them did the same, and she rounded the picnic table to their side. "I don't suppose you'd be willing to come over to Vanguard and hang out there for a while until we formulate the plan."

Alex scratched at the edge of his beanie. "That might be a good idea." He turned.

A car slowed by the curb about fifteen feet from them. The window rolled down.

"Get down!" She tackled Selena, and all three of them went down.

Fire sliced across the outside of Clare's arm. Alex's body jerked.

Selena screamed.

EIGHTEEN

Gage gripped the steering wheel, trying to keep his speed manageable. His lunch break was over, but what he'd discovered in his mom's things was a long overdue find. He couldn't believe that after she'd refused her entire life to talk about his father or where he'd come from, Gage found an original birth certificate with his father's name on it. His real name.

She had to have changed it. Wiped history clean and lived with shutters on anything that could cause her hurt.

He didn't blame her for that. In a way, he'd done the same thing.

But that didn't take away the hurt he'd suffered at her hand, never knowing the truth about his birth.

Alistair McCauley was his father.

Gage didn't know anything about Captain Dennis McCauley beyond the kind of cop he was. If they were related, he didn't know how yet. Could just be a coincidence. It wasn't an unusual name, not like Deluca was.

He squeezed the wheel, heading on autopilot back to the PD the way he'd done so many times. Maybe he'd been living for years like that. Going through the motions. Pretending it didn't bother him that—

His phone rang.

Gage hit the button on the dash screen that showed Sgt. Liam O'Connell was calling. "Yeah."

A second of silence passed. Then, "You okay?"

"Did you call me to ask that?" Gage rarely took lunches by himself. Maybe the boys thought something was wrong.

"No. Shots fired at the park, two hit. The girl was fine, but Clare was hit and so was another guy."

Gage flipped on his lights and siren, then cut across two lanes of traffic to head right. "Is she okay?"

"I don't have details. I just know ambulances took the three of them to the hospital." Liam paused again, just for a second. "Sure you're all right?"

Gage wanted to tell his friend what he'd found. He wanted to say his father's name aloud for the first time in his life. Claim it for himself, no matter what happened. He wanted to know if he could have a relationship with the guy or if he'd end up getting shutdown—shut out—like every other relationship.

"I'm—" He tried to say *fine*, but the word got stuck in his throat.

"You really like this girl," Liam said. "Look—"

"I loved her." Gage gripped the wheel, fighting for focus on what was happening around him more than what swirled in his head. He didn't need an epic crash on the way to the hospital. "And she just *left*. When she was pregnant with my baby."

"Pull over." Liam sounded like he was moving. "We'll come pick you up. Go together and get to the bottom of this. Unless..."

Unless she's dead. Gage sucked in a breath through his

nostrils. "I got it. I'm good." He pulled in a few breaths in a row and pushed them out, slowing the SUV a little so he didn't plow into someone unsuspecting and end up with more problems than he already had right now.

Not going through the motions sucked. He'd become a Christian, and it was like the lights came on. Suddenly he could see things he'd never noticed before, and life seemed so much richer. He had empathy he'd never felt before. Drive to do his job well. Passion to see the people around him succeed. It was exhausting.

Now Clare was back, it was as though someone set off a bomb in his carefully controlled life.

He'd thought there couldn't possibly be more right now than that.

Here he was—metaphorically—reeling from another blow. Finally, after thirty-plus years, he knew who his father was.

Gage pulled into a space at the hospital. He had to push his personal issues aside. Again. Focus on the job. He'd been telling himself that for days, and it would be nearly impossible now.

He strode into the ER.

The desk nurse gaped at him. "Who?"

Gage pulled up short. "Clare Juarez?"

"Oh." Relief washed over her face. "I thought it was a cop."

"Where is she?"

Understanding dawned. "Oh. Three." She pointed.

"Thanks." Gage headed for room three, so much swirling in his mind that he nearly clipped a nurse going the other direction. No one ran in or out of three. In fact, it was pretty quiet.

He spotted her young friend Selena down the hall on a chair. Waiting. Tears in her dark eyes.

Gage slid open the clear Plexiglass door to the room where a doctor bandaged Clare's upper arm. Left side. She wrote with her right, so the injury wouldn't stop her.

On her other shoulder she had the telltale scar of a gunshot wound. On the side of her neck, he spotted a burn scar. Not big, but not nothing. He knew how a lot of wounds felt, but she'd lived a life he'd never experienced.

He might never have met her again.

He walked to the end of the bed and gripped the rail there, squeezing with both hands until his knuckles were probably white.

She's alive. Thank You.

He hadn't wanted to consider the fact she was dead. He'd never get to find out what happened to their child. For the second time in his life he'd have to go through losing her.

Gage wasn't sure how that would've gone down. They didn't exactly get along, but he cared about her. The woman she was now? Clare had turned out to be amazing. He'd like to have her in his life, except all that would do is remind him of everything he would never have because she'd taken it away from him.

"Are you just going to stand there and stare at my feet?"

Gage lifted his gaze.

The doctor grabbed her things. "I'll get the nurse to come in with instructions and discharge papers."

"Thank you." Clare nodded to her.

The door slid shut behind him. Gage swallowed. "Are you okay?"

"You asking me that makes me wonder if I'm not okay, so maybe just don't ask."

She could've died. Gage tried to breathe. "What happened?"

"I had a miscarriage."

It took his mind a second to assimilate what she'd said. "I didn't...," he began. "That's not..." He linked his fingers behind his head and squeezed the back of his neck. "A miscarriage?"

She nodded, the expression on her face full of longing and a whole lot of softness. "The baby died."

Gage's eyes burned hot. He sniffed. "What happened at the park?"

Clare swallowed. She looked to the side and started talking about the robbery crew and how Selena's boyfriend was one of them. He wanted to come in. Talk about what he knew. Then a drive-by.

Gage didn't let go of the bedrail. "He got shot?"

"He's alive. They took him to surgery." She turned on the bed and put her feet down. "I need to see if Selena is all right."

"You're gonna stay here?" He didn't exactly want to leave with everything. Should he hug her?

"Gage."

"Yeah?"

"What are you going to do now?"

"I have to go back to the office." He moved to stand in front of her, but she didn't get up. "But I'm glad you're all right." He reached out, tentatively so he'd know if it wasn't okay, and touched the hair on the side of her face. Brushed it back with two fingers that lingered on her cheek. "I'm really glad you're all right."

Tears gathered in her eyes. "Am I?"

"What do you mean?" He didn't like seeing her this rattled.

"Maybe I seem like I'm all right." She gave him a teary smile. "Maybe it's a front."

"What do you need?"

Clare leaned into his touch for a second, then pulled back. "I'm going to ask my people to call you and let me just be here this afternoon. Okay?"

"You got it." He had no problem running point if she wanted quiet. "Call me if you go anywhere, okay?" For all they knew, she could've been just as much a target as that Alex guy. "Be safe."

Gage touched his lips to her forehead before he left.

NINETEEN

"**D**id they say anything else?"

Selena shook her head. "Just that they'd tell me when he's out of surgery."

Clare didn't question why Selena seemed to be privy to Alex's personal medical information but figured the young woman had told hospital staff they were engaged. She shifted on the hard chair and leaned her head back on the wall, her eyes closed. The bandaged arm had a dull ache to it. They'd given her a shot of something that numbed the pain and threatened to get her to nap even though it was barely three in the afternoon.

"I saw that cop go in your room."

Clare didn't open her eyes. "I don't want to talk about him." She could've called him Gage, or even Lieutenant Deluca. Either one would be telling. Selena was smart enough to notice whichever direction Clare decided to deflect this.

"Getting shot at was crazy."

Clare opened her eyes then, so she could tell Selena she didn't want to talk about this either. Then she saw the look in

Kara's daughter's eyes. "It always is. No matter how many times it happens, you never really get used to it. You just get better at hiding the fear."

"I always thought my mom had no fear." Selena smoothed down the denim over her knee. "Then this one time, we were playing basketball at the park. The ball rolled onto the grass, and I ran to get it. This huge dog ran at me, snarling. She shoved me out of the way, and the owner guy pulled the dog off. She looked at me." Selena sniffed. "I'll never forget her face."

Clare squeezed Selena's hand, then let go.

"I should get some coffee." Selena stood. "Want anything?"

"Same. Thanks."

Selena left her sitting there. Head still against the wall, her behind going numb. The weight of past and present on her shoulders. She'd told Gage what happened. Maybe it hadn't been the right time, but why drag it out any longer?

Now he knew the truth.

She'd honestly figured he would be angry about it. Or at least disappointed. Instead, he'd turned into this caring guy who reached out to comfort her. Even if he considered it a small way, it hadn't felt small to her. That was the most physical affection she'd received in years. Not perfunctory, or a greeting. He'd done it because they shared something huge and painful between them.

Maybe anger would've been better. She found it more difficult to deal with the man he was now than if he got mad at her.

She'd been mad at herself for so long.

"Hey."

Clare blinked and looked up.

Instead of Selena, Ember stood in front of her—all blond

curls and a big smile, carrying Cassie in a baby seat. She set the baby down in front of Clare and took the seat beside her.

Clare leaned down and ran a finger over the sleepy baby's hand. "Appointment for you, or for her?"

"Despite the amount of time she and I have spent here the past few months, neither."

Clare glanced over.

"One of Gage's guys called Trey. Trey called me." She looked at Cassie, pure innocence on her face. Given she'd been a CIA agent, Clare didn't believe one ounce of it.

"So everyone thinks I need you to come over and babysit me?"

"More like they all care and thought you might need someone." Ember shot her a look.

Clare returned it. "That's worse than babysitting."

Ember rolled her eyes. "Don't make me interrogate you. I know some scary stuff."

"And you'd use it on me."

"Now I have new-mom creativity. You ever change a diaper that exploded *everywhere*? Talk about enhanced inter-rogation techniques. One whiff of that and I'd start talking just to get out of there."

Clare had been all spooled up to tell her that no, she'd never dealt with a diaper explosion. But by the end of Ember's speech that had burned out. Clare sat back in the chair. "We got shot at. One of the bank robbery suspects is in critical condition."

"Sure, sure. Anyway, *Gage Deluca*." Ember's eyes were amused, even though she played it cool. "And your history."

"I told him. He didn't get mad."

Ember stayed quiet for a second. "There's more to it than that. Keep talking."

Clare told her how he'd been expecting her to talk about

the shooting, and his entire reaction all the way to him kissing her on the forehead.

"Okay so, I love him."

Clare glanced over.

"I love Trey, don't get me wrong. But this guy?" Ember fanned her face with one hand.

"All right. You're laying it on a little thick."

"You already know you guys work."

"Getting pregnant at seventeen doesn't mean it worked." Clare paused. "Some people even think that's like the *worst* thing someone can do when they're not married." She'd seen atrocities, and some of the most terrible things a person could do to another. Getting pregnant outside of marriage didn't measure up to that.

"What I mean is that you cared about each other."

Clare couldn't argue with that.

"So God is doing something." Before Clare could say anything, Ember continued, "That's why you're here and he's here right now. Why it's hard, because you're both having to face things you buried for a long time."

"I don't have to face it. I lived it." A nurse wandered by, so Clare waited until she was out of earshot. "Gage is the one who broke things off with me. I went through all of it, by myself."

Ember blinked, her eyes wet.

"I don't need your pity."

"It's not pity," Ember said. "It's what God does, when He takes your hard heart and exchanges it for one that's soft."

"That's the last thing I need."

Ember chuckled. "I thought so too, but honestly it's not our choice. I mean part of it is being so exhausted from the heart transplant and being a mom all of a sudden. But also it's His heart for people."

"Why would I want to cry all the time?"

"Well, I can see why you might not want to." Ember swiped a tear from under her eye. "But maybe we should... care a little more for other people."

Clare held up a hand. "Gross."

Ember started to laugh. "Oh, this is gonna be good."

"I don't need to be fixed."

"Sure you do. Everyone is a mess. I see how much you care for Selena and the others like her."

Clare shrugged her healthy shoulder, even though her heart wasn't in it. "He knows what happened now. Gage has his answer, so we can get on with the case. I can work from this end, with Alex and Selena. He can worry about evidence and warrants."

He might've wanted to comfort her after she shared, and she was pretty sure he'd been worried something happened to her. But that didn't mean he wanted to be something to her.

"There isn't going to be anything personal between us," Clare stated—for herself as much as for Ember. "I'm going to focus on what's real and right in front of me. Not on an impossible dream that died a long time ago."

Ember studied her, that blue gaze roaming Clare's face.

Whatever she wanted to say, Selena interrupted when she strode back over, holding two coffees. "The doctor said Alex woke up."

Clare stood, taking the coffee Selena offered.

Her team at Vanguard would rise to the occasion, and she had no doubt they'd do an exemplary job. Clare was going to focus on Selena and what she and Alex had in front of them on top of Alex's recovery from being shot.

"We need to get him a lawyer," she said.

Selena started to shake her head. "He has money. That's not the problem."

When she didn't elaborate, Clare said, "Don't worry. I know exactly who it should be."

TWENTY

Gage stared at the computer screen.

"Hey, that guy—" Liam began.

Gage looked over to where he stood at the door to their office.

He'd been sitting here staring at the monitor, trying not to think about Clare. About their baby. Praying, because he knew with a certainty he didn't quite understand that the child was in heaven. He had hope he would see the baby again, and the feeling was bittersweet.

He'd decided on a whim to look something up, and now he had even more churning in his mind.

At least Clare, Selena, and Alex were safe at the hospital. He'd requested two officers be posted on their floor just to be certain.

Gage glanced over at the clock. "How is it nearly end of shift?"

"You gonna quit and go home?" Liam wandered over.

"No, but—"

"Why are you looking at Captain McCauley's personnel file?"

Gage winced. *Because I didn't think to hide it from you.* "No reason." He clicked the mouse and closed the window. Right now he wasn't quite ready to talk about the fact his birth certificate—at least, the copy his mom had from either before or after she changed it to the version he'd always known—said Alistair McCauley was his father.

A man also listed as Captain Dennis McCauley's next of kin. His father.

Which meant, as far as Gage could tell, the captain was his older half-brother.

"What's going on?"

Gage shook his head. "When there's something to share, you know you'll be the first to know."

"I better." Liam studied him the way he did when he had to figure out a puzzle. Too bad he had no pieces on this one.

Gage stood. "What did you come in to tell me?"

"That guy from Vanguard is here."

"Peter Olson."

"Is he really Freya's brother?" Liam asked.

Gage nodded. They'd all heard about her father, a local do-gooder who ran a halfway house and turned out to be behind a trafficking operation in Benson and stretching all the way to Malaysia.

"He said they have something."

Gage headed out into the main room, where Peter had already plugged his laptop into the port under the table. He tapped keys faster than Gage had ever typed, and the monitor screens on the wall all went black. "Make yourself at home."

Peter grinned, his attention on his laptop screen. "Don't mind if I do." He hit Enter and the monitor screens flashed up with photos. All except the end one, which appeared to be the PD facial recognition system they used. He was running each of the images he had showing on the screens through the DMV—after which he'd probably run the search nationwide.

Blake and Jasper came out of the kitchen, each carrying two mugs. They handed one each to Gage and Liam.

Blake said, "Who are these guys?"

"Did you ask our guest if he wants coffee?" Gage also wanted to know where Dakota was.

Blake reached into the side pocket of his cargos and pulled out a can of sugar free soda—but with all the caffeine. "Couldn't carry all three."

"Thanks." Peter set the can beside his laptop. "Each of these nine men—given Clare said none of them is female, or even possibly female—are possible matches for the suspects. Until Alex wakes up and he can ID them for sure…"

He trailed off for half a second, long enough for Gage to say, "Let's try and eliminate at least some of them as possible suspects."

"Since Alex was one, and there are five, that means four of these nine men are potentially on the crew." Peter glanced over at the screens, to the side and behind him. "If we can ID them, we can gather background information. They're all pros at social media and apparently that involves being nearly completely anonymous."

"They can hide their real names?"

Peter nodded. "It might take some time to figure out who they are if they're not in the local DMV database."

Gage figured it wasn't that Vanguard couldn't run a photo and get a name. They likely had ways to do that. More it was probably the fact they were working with the police on this one, so everything had to be above board.

Liam wandered over to look closer at the screens. "Where'd you get these images?"

"Social media. Selena gave us Alex's phone so we could

access all his accounts, his DMs and the messaging apps he uses." Peter's computer chimed, and he started typing. "We compiled these images through accounts he interacts with, people he talks to in messages using algorithms for particular words or groupings of expressions. We filtered that with a few different things, including how comfortable he is with them. Like if the language he uses is polite or familiar."

"Huh." Jasper came around the desk to look over Peter's shoulder. "That's cool."

The door to the bathroom swished open and Dakota emerged, sniffing and running his fingers through his hair. "What's going on?"

Gage bit back what he wanted to say. "IDs on the suspects."

"Got any?" Dakota glanced around. "I'm gonna pour a cup of coffee."

"Sure." Gage asked Peter, "Any indication from social media if any of them are locals? I know Alex lives just outside Benson, in the hills."

Peter nodded. "He's got a Washington license, and a Benson address." He tapped keys, and it came up.

Jasper said, "What about siblings, or high school classmates?"

"No siblings." Peter glanced at Jasper. "He went to high school in Benson. We should be able to get their yearbook and compare photos. Good idea."

"It's why they pay me the big bucks." Jasper grinned, then took a sip of coffee.

Considering his father was a state senator, and he'd grown up in a mansion in the hills around town, Gage knew for a fact he wasn't in this for the money. When he'd asked Jasper why he became a cop, all he said was that it ticked off his father. Seemed like more than that at the time.

Gage's phone buzzed in his pocket. He tugged it out and saw a text from Clare. "Alex is out of surgery. He should be awake soon."

Peter nodded. The system started to spit out possible matches.

"Send me the photos and any IDs you have. I'll go talk to Alex," Gage said. "Any indication whether they're selling the diamonds locally or elsewhere?"

"We've got some chatter about a sale taking place in Portland. Two Vanguard operatives were dispatched to check it out." Peter shrugged. "Nothing online or in Alex's messages about anything upcoming."

Gage figured that would have shut off the minute they tried to shoot him at the park. "What about threats to Selena?"

Peter's eyes flashed. "We're monitoring the situation. We have it handled, and she'll be protected."

Gage figured Clare could protect herself, but he also planned to watch out for her just in case. "What about anything Alex's messages that smelled like a threat? A reason he might've been targeted?"

"Nothing giving us reason to believe the crew was behind the shooting."

Liam said, "But they are tying up loose ends."

Gage didn't like the sound of that. "I'm headed to the hospital now to check on things." He grabbed a radio and his keys. "Let me know if anything kicks off."

He drove his car from the motor pool just in case he had to respond to a callout. Technically their SWAT team wasn't supposed to work tonight. But tell that to their open cases.

Gage parked in a law enforcement reserved space outside the hospital and headed up to the floor number Clare gave him.

The elevator doors opened to her standing there waiting for him.

"Hey."

Gage stepped off. "You okay?"

"Yeah, I just didn't expect you until tomorrow." She seemed almost nervous.

"Something happening?" Last he'd seen her she'd been injured and at least partly in shock. What had happened since he went back to work? His entire existence had been upended —along with everything he believed about himself—but he didn't know what changed for her.

Clare started walking down the hall, so he kept pace beside her.

He'd kissed her forehead the last time he'd seen her, right after she told him how she'd lost the baby. He still didn't understand why she couldn't have told him, but it was what it was. Years had passed.

Gage lifted two fingers to the cops on the door. Both nodded, the uniformed partners not moving from their posts.

Clare touched his arm. She stopped him beside a door and winced. "Maybe you could hang out here for a second. I just have to go do something."

He stared at her. "You have to go do something?"

TWENTY-ONE

C lare winced. This wasn't good. They'd descended into repeating each other's questions, which meant they weren't communicating at all. "Can we go back to before, when you..."

Nope. She didn't need to go there.

His confusion turned to something a whole lot different. "When I kissed you?"

"It was a peck on the forehead. You call that a kiss?"

Gage glanced at the two officers on duty outside the room. Both intently listening. She didn't want to face this. She wanted nothing to do with it—with him. But Ember's words hung in her head.

Clare had to make a choice.

Right in front of her was the chance to repair the past and have everything she'd ever wanted. But how could she take that step when it might fall apart into nothingness. It might not work, and she'd be left destroyed all over again. Maybe even worse this time.

The alternative? She would not even try. Instead of being

hurt, she'd go back to the cold loneliness of keeping her hard heart just because it was easier than taking the risk.

"I need to go back to the elevator." Clare wasn't going to admit he wasn't the one she'd been waiting for. "I'll be back in a few minutes. Maybe you can check in with your people."

Preferably in a side room, for about half an hour. Which wasn't going to happen.

She stepped back and started to turn away.

"Hold up a moment," a man said. Lieutenant Deluca, judging by the tone of his voice. "What's going on?"

Why fear shuddered through her just then, she had no idea. She was a grown-up. A veteran. A businesswoman and former covert operative. The idea that her teenage boyfriend might come face-to-face with her mother made her want to run away.

"Clare?"

She spun to the female voice. "Hey, Mom."

Gage stiffened.

Clare strode to her mother, who wore a formfitting but professional dress, and kissed her on the cheek. "Thank you for coming."

"My question still stands."

Clare turned back to him, which wasn't better than her mother's assessing gaze. Probably Letitia Juarez had a million questions about Gage, and this whole situation, but she had come anyway. She'd jumped in her sports car and driven from Seattle to Benson just because Clare asked.

"What's going on?" Gage folded his arms.

"My mother has agreed to be Alex's lawyer."

He cleared his throat. "I should speak to Selena and get an update from the doctors."

"She's in there with him, and I think the doctor is in there, too."

One of the officers said, "He is. Selena said Alex should wake up from the anesthetic soon."

Her mother headed for the door.

"Letitia." Gage nodded.

She stared at him for a second. "Lieutenant." Then she went into the room.

Clare wanted to sink into the closest chair, but she forced her knees to lock. Why did being around her mother make her feel fifteen again? Or like the high school senior who'd gotten pregnant. Whose boyfriend had left her to deal with it alone, dropping off the map. Cutting her loose so soon after she told him that he practically left skid marks on his way out the door.

"I wanna talk to her more than that," Gage said.

Clare refused to let on how close she was to a breakdown. It had been a tense day, and it wasn't over yet. She was just nearer the edge than normal—that was all. "I'm sure she'll let you interview Alex. She's a tough lawyer, but there's no reason for him to keep his mouth shut when talking could get him a reduced sentence."

"That isn't what I want to talk to her about."

Before she could ask what on earth he'd want to say, an alarm overhead blared. The door whipped open, and her mother held it. Two nurses rushed in, responding to the problem.

Letitia turned back to the room. "Come on, Selena. Let's give them some room." She held the younger woman's arm and led her out into the hall.

One of the cops said, "What happened?"

Clare frowned. "I'd like to know as well."

Selena's face had paled, and she looked back to the room. When a nurse went to shut the door, Gage stuck his foot there. "Just worry about your patient."

She didn't have time to argue.

Clare realized he'd done it so Selena could see what was happening with Alex. Selena's boyfriend lay in the bed, now completely flat. They hooked up more monitors to him. One of the nurses squeezed air into Alex's lungs. The other stood by the readings, stating what she saw there. The doctor called out orders, then pushed something through the IV in Alex's arm.

"He was coming around."

Clare reached for Selena's arm, and the young woman held on.

"The doctor gave him medicine through the IV that was supposed to help him stabilize and regain consciousness all the way. Then his eyes rolled back in his head, and he started having like a seizure or something." Selena gasped and looked at Clare. "Is he gonna be okay?"

"I don't know, honey."

Beyond Selena, Letitia stared at them. As if she should be surprised Clare had people she cared about and looked out for. This was such a revelation to her? They weren't best friends. Her relationship with her mother was stilted, but since she didn't spend much time with her, that was likely a lack of familiarity.

They weren't friends—they were mother and daughter.

"Okay, give him a second." The doctor took a step back.

The nurses stopped what they were doing. One said, "He's stabilized."

"Keep an eye out. Make sure it stays that way." Through the open doorway she saw the doctor turn from the staff to them—visitors who had all gathered. "Alex came through the surgery, and we were optimistic for his full recovery, but there appears to have been a complication. He's slipped into a coma."

Selena flinched. "What did you give him?"

The doctor frowned. "I don't know what you mean. We administered drugs to try and wake him, but he's at least stable right now."

Selena shook her head. "You gave him something. He was waking up, and whatever you gave him caused this." She pointed at her boyfriend, lying unconscious in the hospital bed.

"Sometimes things like this just happen," Clare said. "They make no sense, but it isn't anyone's fault."

"Unless it is." Selena's expression hardened.

"Let's go talk through what happened." Clare's mother waved Selena to the side. "Then I'll speak with hospital administration. If there's fault to find here, you can have no doubt we'll figure out who is to blame."

The doctor looked at Clare, like she could fix the situation for him.

"Don't look at me." She shrugged. "I wasn't in there, so I don't know what happened."

"I didn't put that man into a coma. No matter what someone with zero medical training and zero grasp on the situation thinks." He strode away and muttered, "Ridiculous."

Gage scrubbed both hands down his face. He turned to the open door, watching the one remaining nurse checking Alex's vitals—or whatever she was doing.

Maybe that doctor was right, even if his bedside manner in conversation with the next of kin had been lousy. She didn't blame him for not appreciating being accused of malpractice. But she also didn't think this was simply about Selena reacting purely on emotion.

The doctor had a phone to his ear now, down the hall. He glanced over at her, then disappeared into a side room.

What stuck with her was the look on his face.

She followed after him, needing to get to the bottom of

this—for Selena as much as for Alex. Considering her mother had been killed, it was up to Clare to take care of her. That might mean removing Letitia from the situation if she stirred up Selena into a lawsuit just to line her own pockets—or whatever reason she had for taking on underdog cases.

"Clare." Gage's footsteps came after her down the hall. Even just the sound of his uniform boots on the floor sounded agitated.

She didn't look back. What was the point? He seemed to think he had a right to be mad, but she'd told him the truth. There was nothing more to say about it.

Clare pulled open the door to the room the doctor had gone in.

He was on the phone, bent slightly forward with a look of anguish on his face. "I did what you asked. Now let her go."

"What's—"

She elbowed Gage. Just a reflex.

The doctor spun to see them in the doorway. "Let her go."

Gage shifted past her and said, "Hang up the phone."

The doctor lowered it. "He's already gone."

TWENTY-TWO

G age stared at the doctor. "You harmed your patient intentionally?"

He couldn't believe Selena's assertion was correct, but only because everyone knew doctors took an oath to do no harm. They were supposed to protect the people under their care. Not be the ones targeted as the one that could be used to get to the patient.

To kill them.

The guy's ID badge said *Preston Mares*. He had styled blond hair and looked like he ran regularly. Gold watch, nicer than the one Jasper wore when he left the PD at the end of shift. "They took my wife. They said they'd kill her if I didn't follow their instructions perfectly." He sniffed, fear in his brown eyes. "I didn't hurt that young man. I just put him in a coma."

"Right." Gage pulled out his phone and sent a specific SOS text to Sargent O'Connell. "Give me your phone. I want to see all communication between you and them."

His phone buzzed. Jasper and Blake were on their way. Liam would hang back at the office with Dakota and wait for whatever he needed that was on the computer. If the time came that they all needed to roll, each one of them would be ready.

He lifted his gaze to Mares. "Who is it? Do you know their name?"

The doctor shook his head. "His voice is disguised. I don't even know if it's a guy."

"When did they take your wife?" Gage remained vaguely aware of Clare still in the room, but so frustrated about that whole thing—and her mom's appearance—he needed to block her out in order to focus. What was important right now was an innocent victim. Two, if he included Alex and the condition their witness was in right now.

Would he survive?

He'd worry about Ms. Juarez and their history later. Gage intended to clear it up, but right now there was a case to work. The past had waited long enough to get resolved, so it could wait another few days.

Kind of like everything else personal swirling around him.

Gage stuffed it down, trying to give it over to the Lord like he was supposed to do. All so he could do his job and not get dragged under by everything Clare's appearance in his life had brought back to the surface.

He was supposed to trust in the Lord rather than lean on his own understanding.

Maybe it worked. Maybe he focused enough it only seemed like it did. Either way, he was able to say, "Doctor Mares. When did they take your wife?"

"I don't know." Mares gasped. "I got this text earlier. I tried to call her, but her office said Katrina never came back from lunch."

"So this all went down fast, then." Clare moved closer to his side.

Gage *almost* managed to keep it from affecting him. Mares handed over the phone with the image full screen. The wife—presumably—tied up, fear in her eyes. Hair disheveled. "Did they give any instructions?"

The photo itself didn't give him much as far as background to work with. Dark and blurry, he couldn't make much of anything out. He tapped out of the photo and back to the message thread. Noted down the number in a text to Liam.

"I thought it was a prank. Or some kind of spam, phishing so they could hack my accounts." Mares sniffed back tears.

The text read,

NO COPS OR SHE DIES. AWAIT CALL WITH INSTRUCTIONS.

Clare read it over his shoulder. "How long before they called?"

"A couple of minutes."

"The same number you got this text from?" Gage asked.

"Yes," Mares replied.

Gage confirmed that was the number he'd been on a call with when they found him in here. "What did they say on the phone just now?"

"I said he wasn't going to tell anyone anything." Mares gasped. "He just kept saying, 'Is he dead?' And I kept telling him that young man wasn't in a condition to tell anyone anything."

"You did the right thing." Clare squeezed his shoulder.

Gage spun around. "Calling the police and reporting a kidnapping would've been the right thing. Not to mention the fact this guy just jeopardized his whole medical career."

The fallout of this would be catastrophic for the doctor, and could be that or worse for Alex, depending on what Mares had given him.

Mares stumbled back and slumped onto a twin bed. This

had to be a room where the staff came to take naps during long shifts. Like the reward for being exceptionally smart, working harder than most careers and hundreds of thousands of dollars of student loans was a job where you had no life and little free time. Didn't seem like a good trade-off to him.

Gage sent the image and screenshots of the message, plus a screenshot of the doctor's call history, over to Liam so he could run the numbers and see what he could get from the picture. "You said she never showed up for work after lunch?"

Mares nodded.

"Did they put her on the phone at all?"

"You mean, like proof of life?"

Gage nodded. "Have you spoken to your wife at all since she was kidnapped?"

"No." Mares shook his head. "Is that bad?" He glanced between Gage and Clare. "Does that mean she's dead?"

Clare pushed out a breath. "Until we know for sure, let's trust she's useful to them so they have her alive. After all, if they killed her you'd have no reason to do what they say." She glanced at him. "The people in my Kidnap and Ransom team are out of the country right now. It would take too long to get them off the job they're working and divert them back here."

She worked her mouth back and forth as though considering it.

"Right. You have that K&R team."

Clare shrugged. "Not that it helps right now."

Gage's phone buzzed. "Let's go out to the hall."

He held the door and spotted Blake and Jasper shaking hands with the uniformed officer watching Alex's room. The other had followed Selena to protect her. Not that it had done any good when the doctor had been the source of the threat.

He caught them up on what had happened.

Jasper winced, but it was short-lived. "We'll do everything we can to get her back. You can be sure of that."

Blake's steady gaze took in the tension between Gage and Clare. "We can take Doctor Mares to the station. Go through everything and see if we can find where his wife is being held."

Gage nodded. Blake had downplayed it, and the doctor wasn't technically under arrest until he was read his rights. Before that happened, he'd be treated as a cooperating witness. The district attorney would decide if they were going to bring charges for what he'd done to Alex.

It meant walking a fine line, but they needed all the information available in order to make an arrest. And they had to find Mares' wife. Alive if at all possible.

Gage didn't want to consider the likelihood she would be killed, but the truth was, it remained a higher probability than their finding her safe and sound.

"Vanguard will assist, of course." Clare nodded to him, then the doctor.

Of course she thought that.

"This is a police case," Gage said. They hardly needed her people confusing things when her division that worked cases like these wasn't even available.

With the time crunch he had to fall back on what he knew. His team, and the training they'd done together. He had to do what he knew because that was how he'd been trained. Procedure and training meant he could control the variables.

Clare? She was the unknown here. The risky proposition because he couldn't work out the end result. It meant taking a chance, and he wasn't sure he wanted to do the risky thing.

Even if jumping in with both feet and having her in his life meant he gained everything he'd ever wanted.

And this time, he might not lose it all.

"SWAT can take it from here." He wasn't backing down about that.

Regardless of the hurt that flashed across her face at being sidelined. She'd realize soon enough it was better for her to stay here. Safeguard Alex and Selena. Work the case from this end, praying another doctor could reverse what Mares had done.

The doctor started to go with Blake and Jasper, but his phone chimed, stopping him in his tracks. "It's them." He looked at Gage. "They're leaving her for me to go get her."

"Do they say when or where?"

Mares' face paled. "Freemont Park. Eight p.m."

Gage looked at his watch. "We have three hours."

TWENTY-THREE

Berlin walked out of his room, closing and locking the door behind him. The master, of course. The others bunked together in smaller rooms, but he had his own because it was his house. And he had another suite of rooms.

Miami and London were both taken care of. Retrieval of the diamonds was in the works.

He forced his body to gasp. Worked his way up into what would appear to be a freaked-out state. Then he strode out to the living area way too fast.

Rio and Phoenix were occupying themselves sniffing more up their noses. Drinking. Passing the time the only way they knew how when the job was done and their worthless lives no longer meant anything.

He had no use for them.

The gun tucked in the back of his belt pressed against the skin of his back. How easy it would be to pull it out and bury a bullet in each man's forehead.

"I'm going out."

Rio twisted around, face pale and eyes red rimmed. The guy looked like a corpse.

Berlin had to keep himself from wincing in disgust.

Rio said, "Did you hear anything?"

Berlin shook his head. "I might try and call that girl of his. Selena, is that her name? I need to try and track her down. Ask her if she knows where he is."

"It doesn't make sense that he'd just ditch us." Phoenix actually teared up. "This whole thing is falling apart, and we're not even done!"

They were done. "It's gonna be okay, yeah?" He'd rather have killed himself right then. "Pull it together and trust me."

They either did, or he would kill them right now.

Rio nodded like a little puppy. It really was a shame, since it seemed Miami was the one he could actually tolerate. "We trust you. Just one more thing, right? We heard what you were doing upstairs."

Berlin stilled.

"It's fine, right? You got this?" Rio locked eyes with him. "When you're done, we can split the money and go our separate ways."

The two of them should check into rehab with the money.

Berlin nodded. "I'll call you again in the future if I need help. You guys are good." He tried to look sincere. "No one else I trust more than I trust the two of you."

Phoenix leaned one arm on the back of the couch. "Shame about Miami."

Berlin drew on more sincerity for that one. "I gotta go do a thing, yeah? You guys know what you're doing later?"

They both nodded.

"Good. Don't worry, okay. And don't go in my room."

He grabbed the Subaru keys and drove across town to a brand-new top-of-the-line laundromat. Close to a few new apartment complexes. He'd have to think about getting a condo or something in Calgary—once he got there.

Something legit, unlike this place that was a front for an Estonian family with ties to a crime lord in their home country. The wife's uncle.

He headed in the front door, hood up and sunglasses on, walked up to the counter, and laid down the ticket stub. "Picking up an order."

The clerk looked at the stub, then waved over his shoulder. "Second on the right."

Berlin checked no one watched, then headed through the swinging door to the back hall. The sign above would make anyone think he'd asked where the bathroom was.

He knocked on the second door, then let himself in.

The man behind the desk wore a polyester suit and far too many gold rings. He had more hair on his hands than on the top of his head. The wife—or girlfriend, or whatever this one was—sat at a desk to the right. Tiny, leggy, and blonde. She barely spoke English.

Christoph grinned because Berlin paid him so much, why wouldn't he be happy? "I have your papers." He hauled himself out of the chair and slid the file cabinet open. Two pieces of paper. Birth certificate, high school graduation. Out of a wall safe he pulled a driver's license for British Columbia and a Canadian passport.

Berlin felt a spark of excitement set alight in him.

Christoph had done it. *So I don't need him anymore.*

Berlin pulled the gun from the back of his belt and shot the Estonian in the chest, then head. He spun around and shot the woman in her face even while she screamed.

She was moving when the round hit her, so he had to fire another. She spun with the force of it, clipped the desk going down, and made a mess on the carpet.

Berlin swiped up the papers, passport, and license, then took the stack of cash from the wall safe and used a backpack on a hook to stuff it all inside. He strode the opposite way down the hall, to the rear exit. Hit the bar. Jogged down the pavement.

Ditched the car.

He ran two miles before he felt the urge to pat the pocket that should contain the diamonds but didn't.

I'll kill you.

Only one more thing to do.

TWENTY-FOUR

Clare shifted in the front seat of her car, one of the generic ones Vanguard kept so operatives could drive something unassuming that couldn't be traced back to them. She made a fist and rubbed it on the leg of her running pants, shorts over leggings.

The evening held a chill. Mares' wife wasn't supposed to be here for two hours, but it wasn't like she'd never sat and waited for someone to show.

Her mind wanted to run the highlight reel of the last day of Kara's life, but she refused to allow her mistakes to eclipse everything. The way Kara's blood had pooled on the sand. Hot and sticky. No matter how much Clare had tried, her friend didn't make it.

Mission success.

When they'd given up so much in casualties? Clare hadn't been able to stomach labeling that mission a win even if they'd brought the target home. The faith she'd had in the military died that day. She'd walked away from the army, realizing she'd tried having faith in the guy she loved. In the future they were supposed to have—the life they created.

That hadn't worked.

She'd tried having faith in her mother.

Then the army.

Now all she had was Vanguard, regardless of whatever Gage was trying to do now. Clare knew what she could do. The strength she had to go after what she wanted. How she wouldn't ever let her company fail, or let her people down.

All she had was herself.

It was why she hadn't allowed herself to get into a relationship with anyone since Anthony. He'd been a doctor, a lot like Doctor Mares. A guy with more flash than substance. A genius at his work—and who left her to hers when he got absorbed in his career and building his name. It had worked for a while. She wouldn't say their two-year marriage ever succeeded.

Eventually he'd come clean that he was in a relationship with a colleague.

The fact it had been a hassle to take off work for the day just to show up in court for the divorce told her all she needed to know.

She hadn't had any heart in that relationship. For a long time, she hadn't had heart about anything. Maybe it died with her baby. When that life slipped from her and she'd broken—both in her heart, and aloud. Alone in the bathroom. No one but her and the life she'd been responsible for.

Clare wondered if she'd felt anything since.

A woman with a stroller walked by the front of her car and headed down the walking path that circled the outside of the expanse of green that made up the center of Freemont Park. Three acres, surrounded by trees that almost disguised the fact they were practically in the middle of downtown Benson.

She'd always loved this city. Even when she'd lived for a year closer to Seattle, those months spent in her mother's cabin. She'd finished high school there. But as soon as she got out of the army she knew where she wanted to go.

She just hadn't expected Gage to be here.

Clare's phone rang. *Mom.* She reached for where it was clipped up to the left of her steering wheel on the dash and slid her finger across the screen before she tapped the button for speakerphone. "Hi, Mom."

"Honey." Her mother let out a breath, as though that were a whole statement or question on its own. Maybe it was.

"You're gonna have to be more specific if you want to talk about something." Clare didn't have time to decipher whatever her mother had to say.

"Gage Deluca. That has to be hard."

Clare made a face because her mother couldn't see her— and neither could anyone else.

The police wouldn't be here until closer to the time the doc's wife was supposed to be left. Traded back. She didn't like it when a woman was a bargaining piece. Ever.

She sighed. "Mom, it is what it is. I didn't expect him to show up in my life." Now that he had, however...

"You knew I'd see him?" Her mother paused. "So you wanted things to come to a head? To force a confrontation."

"That's not what this is. Alex needed representation, and I'm guessing Selena could use counsel."

"And I should invoice Vanguard for this, or you'll be paying out of your own pocket?"

Clare would pay either way with those options—and she'd do it for Selena. Still. "Alex and Selena can both afford your bill. Whatever rate you put them on. They're famous social media stars."

"I know, Clare. I did my research."

There *was* something she could ask her mother. "What really happened with Gage when he broke up with me? I mean, he freaked out and left after I told him about the baby." She'd convinced herself, in her teenage naïveté, that he'd just been overwhelmed. "I saw when he came back. I looked out the window, so I know you talked to him even though you said he left."

"And?"

Clare gripped the door handle, just to ground herself. She stared at trees, swaying in the breeze. "He turned away after whatever you said. He saw me in the window. Shook his head and said, 'No way.' What was that, Mom?"

Her mother had ordered her to pack her bags. They'd headed to their family cabin, where they had no cell signal. Not that phones were even that functional back then. Calls and barely text messages. Certainly no camera or internet. Her mother had told her the cabin landline was out of service.

They'd been completely cut off.

"He wasn't worthy of you. Of the child you would bring into the world." Her mother sighed. "I'm sorry for how that turned out, but it really was for the best. Your life didn't need to be derailed by a mistake."

Clare wasn't sure, even in her darkest anguish, if she'd ever considered it to be a mistake. "I can't do this right now." She hung up, done with the conversation.

For years Clare had been the one who felt not worthy. When her baby had died. When her teammates had given their lives for her, and the success of the mission. Clare had walked away wondering why it always seemed like someone else had to die. Why not her?

She shoved open the car door, gasping for air.

Frustrated energy ran through her from sitting too long. Rolling around all these emotions she'd buried. The last thing she needed was to be cooped up. She holstered a pistol under her arm and zipped up her jacket over it.

Running clothes. Sneakers that admittedly saw more gym time than streets or mountain trails. She pulled her hair back in a ponytail and stowed her phone in the pocket on the side of her leggings.

Clare locked her car and joined the people in the park enjoying the spring weather and a break in the rain for one day before another front blew in.

She sprinted at first, just to burn off the energy that wouldn't dissipate. The running dialog in her mind that she was alive and others had given their lives, and it made no sense that the worthless one lived while those with honor died and the world lost their light.

Makes no sense.

There was supposed to be order in the world. Otherwise she wouldn't crave what it could bring her. The peace she would feel when everything made sense.

Clare ran so hard her heart pounded in her ears, then slowed to a jog.

Someone screamed.

Clare changed directions, veering onto a path off to the right into the trees. The woman with the stroller she'd seen had stopped on the path to watch the brush off the trail. "What is it?" she called out as she jogged over.

"There." The woman pointed and turned a pale gaze at Clare. "Right there."

Clare stopped beside her. Spotted the woman in the brush. Looked back at the mom, with no time to check if the child saw this or was sleeping. "Get out of here. Now."

Doctor Mares' wife lay in the dirt up against a tree.

Clare pressed two fingers to the woman's neck and gasped. *She's alive.*

"A guy was here," the mom said. "He ran off."

TWENTY-FIVE

A kid jumped and tossed the ball. It swished into the net, then bounced, and another one caught it.

"Nice," Gage remarked from his spot on the bleachers.

Jasper would've slapped the back of Gage's shoulder, but he was currently on the far side of the basketball courts near the parking lot. From his spot he could see the kids' pickup game. "But maybe we should make this more interesting. How about two hundred bucks on the winner?"

Blake tensed.

Gage didn't glance over at the far end where the dog area was—he just saw it out the corner of his eye. He spoke into his radio. "Except that we're not off work playing basketball at the park. We're watching for a crew of dangerous thieves."

Jasper muttered something Gage didn't catch over the radio.

Gage couldn't get into what that was right now or the two moms close enough to hear would wonder why he was talking to himself. He'd have to put his phone to his ear and pretend he was on it.

Liam was silent. He'd taken the end of the park too far for Gage to see and was watching both for the suspects and babysitting Dakota. Neither of them wanted to think of it that way, but it was true.

Dakota had been more and more on edge all day. Something was up with the guy, and the last thing they needed was that putting an innocent in danger.

Blake, standing watch at the entrance dog parents used, said, "You know...she was pretty mad when you dissed her at the hospital. What are you gonna say when you see her?"

Gage shifted on the bench, trying to get his vest to quit digging into his side. At least it was cold enough they could have jackets on over their protective gear. People in the park didn't need to see the three of them were armed. He turned his head. "I have no idea. I don't want to talk about Clare."

"What's going on?" Blake glanced around. "You okay, Gage?"

If only Gage could get him to reciprocate and actually let them into his life and what happened when he was off shift. Did it even matter that he knew his father's name after thirty-four years of having no clue where he'd come from?

Captain McCauley just might be his half-brother. They both had lives. The captain had a family. Was it really worth disrupting that out of some selfish desire for connection? Maybe Dennis McCauley didn't want to know Gage might be his brother.

Gage tugged out his phone. "It's not important right now." No notifications. "Once the detectives are done questioning the doc, we'll know more about how this thing is gonna go down."

They still had time. After the doctor's phone had gone off, they'd opted to hand him to other cops for questioning and run this operation themselves. Get here early just in case something happened. All of them would rather be in the field than in the office.

An ambulance siren approached from the west.

Blake said, "Did we get any notifications?"

Jasper pulled out his phone. "I'll text my friend at dispatch. See what this is about."

Gage got up and headed for the end of the bleachers so he could jump down.

Why were all his instincts firing? Instead of blowing off steam before it was time to ready up for the operation, he sensed something was already happening.

Gage pocketed his phone and unzipped his jacket so he could reach his gun fast.

"You see something?" Jasper took a step toward him.

Gage held up his hand. "Hold where you are, but keep your eyes open."

The kidnapper was supposed to leave Mrs. Mares here. That meant they had to bring her—or already had. Dead, her body dumped ahead of time. Alive, shoved out of a car to wander the park until she was located.

A guy ran across the grass wearing normal clothes, not activewear. He ran like a suspect fleeing from a scene rather than someone exercising.

Gage said, "Jeans, blue hoodie. Cut him off, Jas."

"Copy that." Jasper moved from his post.

"Blake?"

"Right behind you."

Gage drew his gun and ran after the guy, moving in on instinct more than anything else. So if this guy turned out to be innocent, they'd have to stand down pretty quickly. No one wanted to target someone just living an upstanding life. That wasn't what the police were supposed to do in the community.

They were meant to uphold the law and protect innocent people.

Jasper approached the guy from in front. "It's one of them." The nine photos Vanguard had come up with, possible suspects.

Gage tore across thirty feet of grass to catch up, speaking into his radio as he ran. "Use caution but detain."

"Copy that."

Before Jasper even finished saying that, the guy darted to the right and bolted. He was fast. Jasper whirled around and slammed into a jogger. They both went down.

Gage jumped a tiny brick wall by the path that intersected the field. Blake ran to his right about ten feet. The two of them raced after the suspect. "Benson PD. Stop!"

The guy kept running.

Gage announced who they were twice more. Ran as fast as he could. He heard Jasper in his earpiece apologize to the guy he'd run into.

The suspect swung his arm back, brandishing a weapon.

Gage squeezed off a shot that went wild.

The crack split the air in the park like the sudden discharge of a firework.

People screamed.

"Get down!" Gage ducked and went to one knee. There was zero cover. "Everyone get down!" The last thing he needed was for an innocent to get hurt.

The guy ran for a collection of cars parked on the street, angled spaces people could pull into and out of quickly. A dark-colored van had been backed up to the sidewalk under cover of some trees.

Dakota sprinted up the sidewalk to Gage's right. He was going to get there first, but not before the guy jumped in and hit the gas.

He pulled out and nearly sideswiped a guy on a motorcycle.

Someone honked.

Dakota drew his gun and aimed at the van.

No.

He squeezed off a shot and hit the van tire.

Gage ran past him. "Stand down!" He raced out into the street after the van, watching to see where it went.

It veered dangerously and careened across the turn lane into oncoming traffic. Someone laid on their horn as they streamed past. The van bumped the curb and headed at the front window of a department store.

Glass shattered. The van broke through siding and crashed into the storefront.

Gage ran to the turn lane and narrowly missed getting hit by a pickup truck. He slowed two steps, waited for the sedan to pass, and held up his hand so no one else tried to run him over.

On the far side of the street, in front of the store, someone jumped out of the window. A woman, flustered and breathing hard. She ran into him.

He grasped her elbows. "Be careful."

The guy climbed out of the van and moved farther into the store.

"Benson PD. Stop! Put your hands up!" He climbed over debris into the store. The chatter in his earpiece registered, and he connected the fact his team were right behind him, taking flanking positions and backing him up.

The guy reached for a woman half lying on the floor and started to drag her to her feet.

"Don't! Stand down and put your hands up!" Gage stared at him, gun aimed. Trying to get a shot.

There was no way he could fire—like Dakota had done—

without putting an innocent in danger. That had been a reckless move. Someone could be dead under the van. Hurt in this store, bleeding out while they took precious moments to detain this guy.

"It's over."

The guy hauled up the woman and held her in front, his gun to the underside of her chin. If he pulled the trigger, half her head would be gone in a split second.

"Don't do this."

"He's right." Clare stepped up next to him. "You don't want to do this."

TWENTY-SIX

C lare took a step forward. "We can talk about this. Figure out a solution that works for all of us."

"I know you." The gunman's expression bored into her for a second, then something behind her drew his attention. One of the SWAT guys moving into position, probably.

She had to admit, it felt good knowing she wasn't alone. Backup wasn't something she'd had much lately. Having an armed elite team of cops with her meant she wasn't unprotected. She could take another step, assured they wouldn't let her get hurt.

Which left it to her to focus on the hostage. Up the chance she'd walk out of this alive.

"Yeah, I was in that bank." Clare held her hands up, her gun still holstered under her jacket. She wouldn't be able to draw it before he shot either the hostage or her. "Why don't you let that woman go and we'll talk about it? Figure out a way you can walk away from this."

His lips curled back. "I don't think so. I'm the one in charge here, and I don't need you interfering."

The woman in his arms whimpered. Blood ran down the side of her face, her eyes glassy from the injury.

"I know you didn't kill that woman in the trees, and you didn't kill the teller at the bank." Clare shrugged a tiny bit. "So far you haven't taken a life. Let's keep it that way."

Gage moved beside her, half a step to the left. Trying to get a better angle so he could maybe shoot the guy in the head. Too risky in her estimation, but she wasn't surprised he would try. That was the kind of cop he was—always thinking about the life he'd save and the result that would accompany it.

No one else would be hurt.

Except Clare.

She'd been waving the EMTs over to the injured, practically dead woman. Trying to pray that the doctor's wife lived. Even if she didn't all the way believe that would work. Or that God would listen to someone like her.

Then she'd heard the gunshot.

Reacting purely on instinct, Clare had raced across the park with her gun out. Seen the commotion on the street and then the crash. That SWAT was in the middle of it had been a relief, but she didn't fully assimilate that until she was in the store. And then she'd seen the woman being held against her will and all thought went out the window.

So here she was.

Gage might not like it, but she would do everything she could to help.

"I'm gonna shoot her." The guy sneered. "Just so you quit meddling."

"She can leave," Gage said. "You and I can talk this out. But you let both women go."

"Or better yet," Clare found herself saying, "let her go and take me instead."

The SWAT guys reacted. Clare wasn't interested if they

didn't like her idea. She just had different tactics than they employed. Her life for years had been war. Far more savage than hometown law enforcement.

"Yeah? So you can talk me to death. Ruin things even more."

The woman whimpered again.

Clare couldn't look at the woman. Not when that would create a connection she'd have to feel if the woman was killed. Right now she just needed to be a faceless innocent victim. "Your crew has a leader. You're two down, and he's scrambling."

"Because of you!"

"Don't make this worse," she said. "Right now your leader is the one with the problem, not you."

Gage shifted, his gun still raised. "Put the gun down and put your hands up."

Clare had to admit she liked standing side by side with him. But it couldn't last. She couldn't let these cops hurt the innocent, which meant she moved in then. Someone made a frustrated noise, low in their throat. She didn't wonder who it was.

"Let her go and take me."

The gunman stared at her, desperation and the gleam of narcotics in his gaze. Too glassy. He had no ability to be rational or calm. "You wanna save her life?" He shifted.

Clare grabbed for the woman when he shoved her away. *He's going to shoot her.* That was how he'd get shot—something he might've seen as his only way out. But they needed the information he could give them.

She held the woman with one hand and kicked at his gun hand with the other. His hand flung up at the force of the impact and he cried out. The gun went flying.

Clare spun with the woman, gathering her up in case

more shots went off. She had to have her body between the gun and the innocent person. *No one else is dying on my watch.*

"Clear!" Gage flipped the guy onto his front. "You're under arrest."

She walked away, clutching the woman while he continued talking. Doing his cop thing. "Let's get you outside. We can have EMTs check you out."

Gage called out, "Blake! Escort the woman outside. Clare, you're not going anywhere." The lethality in his voice made her stop.

She couldn't do anything else when he spoke with that authority.

The officer he'd called Blake, the black guy with REED on a Velcro patch on his vest, took the woman from her. He even offered her a conciliatory look. "This way, ma'am. We'll get you taken care of."

The woman said, "Thank you."

Clare didn't know who she was talking to.

Gage hauled the guy up. "Liam. One for holding."

"Copy that, Lieutenant." O'Connell took the gunman and walked him out.

"Jasper, Dakota, check for anyone else. Make sure no one is injured or worse since you crashed this car into the store." Gage's gaze lit fire in Dakota's direction.

Clare didn't move.

He stalked toward her. "What kind of fool-headed, hair-brained—"

"That's not fair," she protested.

"You could have gotten yourself killed." He stopped almost nose to nose with her. "SWAT just saved your life, even though you were determined to lose it. And that woman could've died if that risk you took didn't work." He shook his head.

This close to her, the past took over. Clare remembered the times they'd been this near each other. Stolen moments that got them in the mess that ended their relationship. Beauty that ended in so much pain when she lost the baby.

"What were you thinking?" He shook his head again. "SWAT had this handled before you even came in."

"In a standoff with a hostage?" She scoffed. "That's not what I call handling it."

"You don't think much of me, do you? Or you wouldn't have thought you could do better. Maybe you wouldn't have walked into the line of fire and tried to take over." His eyes flashed. "You're not the CEO out here, Clare."

She couldn't get past the first thing he'd said. *You don't think much of me.* "I don't think much of a guy who abandons the person he said he'd loved in the worst time of her life." Not that it had much to do with a standoff, but it had to be said.

"I'm not talking to you about that right now."

She huffed. "Because you'll have to admit you were wrong about something."

"That would be better than paying off someone to get out of your life."

She gasped. "What are you talking about?"

"Lieutenant!" Jasper called across the room. "Get another bus. There's an injured man over here."

Gage started to walk away.

"We're not done talking about this."

He glanced back. "You didn't want trash like me in your life." He lifted his hands, then let them fall back to his sides. "What else is there to say?"

His officer buddy, Dakota, stared at her like she was the cause of this instead of him. Clare's ears rang with his statement. *Paying someone off to get out of your life.* What was he talking about? He was the one who'd shaken his head and walked away.

Her life had fallen apart.

Because of him.

TWENTY-SEVEN

G age pointed to a chair. "Get your report written up. I want it all on paper."

Dakota slumped into the chair so that it rolled back. He grabbed the edge of the desk and tugged the chair back in. "So you can use it to hang me out to dry?"

Gage set both hands on the desk and leaned toward his subordinate. "You're lucky someone didn't get killed today because of what you did."

"I stopped that van."

"Only because somewhere in that mixed-up brain of yours you thought going against procedure was the right thing. People were hurt in that store, Officer Masterson." Gage straightened and walked out. Otherwise he would wind up suspending Dakota before he even gave the guy a fair shake.

What he wanted was for Dakota to write up his full report so he could get him on suspension—and seeing the therapist— all without anyone realizing what the rest of SWAT knew.

He didn't even want to think it. But the reality was,

Dakota needed to realize for himself that rehab was where he needed to be right now. Not on the job, putting people's lives in danger.

People who stubbornly got other people killed because they didn't know when to quit were the worst kind. They weren't anything close to being heroes.

Gage didn't want to trust anyone like that.

He headed down the hallway in the cave, to where they'd stashed the gunman in an interrogation room. The fake ID he'd had on him wouldn't give them much of a clue who he was. At least, not until fingerprints came back. If he was in the system.

The cell phone he'd had on him was another story, but the last thing he wanted to do was hand it over to Vanguard Investigations.

After the face-to-face confrontation he'd had with Clare, he didn't want to see her anytime soon. All it would do was drag up their history—again—and air it out like laundry on a drying rack. Like they had when he was a kid, and there hadn't been money to pay for a dryer. Thankfully their ancient washing machine never died. He still used the same one in his house now.

Liam headed from the opposite direction down the hall. "I heard about the conversation you guys had after we took this guy." The sergeant thumbed in the direction of the interrogation room. "Why'd you wait until I left to get into it with Clare?" He grinned.

Gage shook his head. "My personal life isn't for your entertainment."

Liam would have probably put him in a headlock any other time over a comment like that. But right now his eyes widened. "Seriously, bro. What's going on?"

"I need to question our gunman."

"Anything else?"

Gage took a chance on the friendship he had with Liam that went beyond being colleagues and teammates. "I need a current address on Alistair McCauley." Before Liam could ask, he added, "Captain Dennis McCauley's father."

Liam stilled. "I can look it up. I—"

"Good. Thanks." Gage turned away because he didn't want Liam asking follow-up questions. He had the paper files he needed, and it was time to get to the bottom of what was going on.

He pulled open the door to the interrogation room and took a seat across from the young man. Probably in his early twenties, though it seemed he lived hard and played hard. Some people wore the things they had done, and seen, on their face. Others it was in their eyes. "Your driver's license says you're Steven Phoenix, but I'm guessing that's a fake ID."

The guy smirked.

"Nevertheless, Steven, you're the only one in cuffs. That makes you the responsible party for the five of you." Gage flipped open the file. He slid a photo of the burned body from the van across the table. "Make that four. What happened? Why did you decide he needed to die?" He half figured he would say something asinine like, *Snitches get stitches.* As if anyone actually used that expression.

The kid looked at the photo and swallowed.

"Then you nearly killed Alex in that drive-by shooting."

Steven blinked. "Who?"

Gage flipped over the next photo. This one from Alex's driver's license.

"Oh, him." Steven leaned back in the chair. "I heard he was some kind of trick shot YouTube star. Tripping his girlfriend so he could win a wilderness race. All so he could go and face-plant in Arizona." He grinned. "Most hilarious thing I've seen in a long time."

Gage wasn't going to debate the merits of failure being funnier than success, or people finding it more funny when someone hurt themselves. "There were five of you in the bank. You might not have been in the room when the teller was killed, but I'm guessing you were there when the van your friend was in was pushed off the cliff." He paused a second. "Why did he have to die?"

Whatever this guy thought, it might not be the logic behind the actions of the guy in charge and what he was doing. But Gage at least needed to know what he believed was true.

Which made Dakota's actions today even more terrifying. Because if his choices had gotten someone killed, then he was no better than these young guys taking lives and thinking it was no big deal.

He prayed right then that Dakota would have a turn-around. That he would claim responsibility for his actions and sort out his life. Gage couldn't see him having much more of a future with SWAT, but that didn't mean their friendship would ever be over.

He just wanted to have a real conversation with Dakota where he was honest.

"You think I was in the bank?" The guy lifted his chin. "Prove it."

"And when I run the DNA we collected, you're so sure it won't include yours?"

Steven scoffed. "I bank there. Of course you're going to find my DNA. In fact, I'm pretty sure I gave myself a paper cut last time. You might even find blood."

"I'm sure I might." Gage studied him for a moment. "You

have an important choice to make right now. It's come down to you and what happens next."

"I'm not going to talk."

"Then I'm at liberty to charge you for two murders and one count of attempted murder." Gage paused. "You think you're ever going to see the outside of a prison after that?"

"Do it." Steven lifted his chin. "See if I care what happens to me."

"Are they worth you throwing your life away?" Gage waited but said nothing else. "You're within your rights to seek counsel. Might be a smart move."

Steven shrugged. "Come back with a better offer."

Gage stood. "Maybe I will."

He strode out so Liam could take a crack at the guy in a couple of hours. Because sometimes pushing and pushing didn't convince a witness to talk. Better to let him sit and over-think it, come up with worst-case scenarios and eventually decide it was in his best interest to cooperate.

Until he started talking they wouldn't make much sense of this. Unless Alex woke up and was able to ID the other members of their crew.

Someone had to start talking.

He closed the door to the interrogation room, trying not to make it obvious how frustrated he was.

Liam strode down the hall toward him.

Gage didn't like the look on his face. "What?"

"Clare's here."

Everything in him wanted to turn and head the other way. "Did you find that address?"

Liam nodded. "She wants to know what we got from Steven Phoenix so far."

"Text me the address. I need some time, maybe a couple of hours." Until then he was going to keep feeling like the world had flipped upside down. Like everything he'd ever believed now made no sense.

He wanted to go home, take a shower, and not shut it off until the water ran cold.

Or go meet his father for the first time.

TWENTY-EIGHT

Clare walked out of the elevator through the ground-floor hallway in the police department. She could head back upstairs, get a meeting with Russ. Tell him that SWAT had shut her out. Force them to accept her admittance to what they were doing tonight.

Exhaustion hung around her like a cloud.

She needed a meal and a change of scenery. Instead, she lingered too long looking at Kyle's memorial picture hanging on the wall. It wasn't fair to compare Gage and Kyle. One was a lost dream, the other a living nightmare.

Clare didn't know what to do.

Addie, one of the special agents with the small FBI office here, caught her attention as she passed the window, then motioned her into their office. Asking without words if Clare wanted to come in.

She lifted her wrist and tapped her watch. Shook her head. Kept going, outside where she could stretch her legs and inhale the crisp evening air.

Today hadn't exactly been a success, but it also wasn't a complete disaster. The police had one of the suspects in custody. One was dead. Alex would—hopefully—wake up soon. That only left two.

Clare grabbed a chicken salad sandwich and a cup of soup from a drive-through. By the time she was done, she'd decided to talk her way into Mrs. Mares' room and ask her questions. The cops weren't planning on doing that until the morning, after she'd had time to rest. If Clare could get in there tonight and get information, Vanguard's night shift could work while everyone rested, they'd all be one step closer to ending this.

Was that what she wanted?

Gage would probably cut her loose as soon as the case was done. If he hadn't already. Things weren't exactly polite between them, not even for the sake of being professional and cordial. Too much water under that bridge. Bitter water that seemed to want to choke both of them.

She swung by to see Selena on her way to Mrs. Mares' room. Her friend sat beside his bed, reading a magazine.

Clare knocked on the open door. "Hey."

Selena looked up from the open magazine in her lap. She whimpered, tossed the magazine on the chair, and came over. Arms open.

Clare gave her a hug. "How is it going?"

Selena dragged Clare back to the chair and paced while Clare sat. "They think they can reverse what the doctor gave him. That he might wake up soon, maybe tomorrow." She waved her hands up and down. "It's just... I don't..."

"You were gonna break up with him."

"And now he's been shot!" Selena gasped. "How am I supposed to pretend like everything's fine, and then I've got to wait until he's better so I can break it off? Or I just leave him here alone and he wakes up to no one, with no clue what happened."

Clare knew so many people who had married and stayed

with their significant other for years that she'd forgotten breakups were a part of life. Some were amicable, some less so. Hopefully the effects were limited—two people who realized before they were married that it wasn't going to work, like Selena with Alex. Gage had walked away when she'd been pregnant, and his departure devastated her.

"If you feel that way..." Letitia stepped into the room. "Then I'd advise you leave now. When Alex wakes up, he's going to have plenty to occupy him with the pending charges and fighting his case. He'll need all his strength to get through the court case. You being here will only confuse things."

"Mom." Clare stood.

"No, she's probably right." Selena sighed.

Her mother hadn't had a long-term relationship in her life, as far as Clare knew. Maybe she'd had a boyfriend for a few months, but she'd never been married. She worked probably ninety hours a week, and she was excellent at what she did. The trade-off might be a dry personal life, but maybe that was what she wanted out of her life.

"She isn't." Clare knew for sure, even if her life looked a lot like her mother's.

"I'd think you might understand." Letitia shrugged and set her purse on the counter by the tiny sink. "Being a business owner. Why get caught up in emotional turmoil when there's work to be done?"

"What did you say to Gage that made him walk away?" He'd said she offered him money to break it off—whether he thought she was behind it, or her mother.

Letitia lifted her chin.

Selena glanced between them.

Clare put her hand on the younger woman's arm and shook her head. To her mother, she said, "Maybe we should step out into the hallway so we can talk about this." There was an unconscious man lying in hospital bed in the room, after all.

"Why? Gage wasn't the kind of male you deserved in your life."

I was pregnant with his baby. "He was in my life anyway. Part of it."

"All that worked out for the best, though."

"Because I lost the baby?"

Selena gasped.

Clare said, "What did you offer him, Mom? What did you give him to walk away?"

"More than enough." Her mother's face had a guarded expression.

Clare's stomach flipped over. The meal had helped, but now it sat there in her midsection and decided to sour. She swallowed. "You gave him money to leave?"

He'd walked away, shaking his head. Wanted nothing to do with her now that he'd thought over what happened.

He'd comforted her when she told him what happened, when she'd been hurt. He was the kind of man who took care of people when they got knocked down. But as soon as they showed signs of being okay? All bets were off. He went back to his true self and showed his real feelings.

"It's not like he's going to be part of your life." Letitia scoffed.

"You think you did me a *favor*?" Clare said.

And her mother had decided it was the right thing. No one would be able to persuade her otherwise.

"Forget it." Clare turned to Selena, who slammed against her and squeezed Clare with her strong arms. They needed to get in the gym soon. Keep up their strength and Selena's skills. "Call me if you need anything."

Selena nodded against her shoulder. "Thanks."

"And get some rest, even if you come back tomorrow so Alex doesn't wake up alone." Clare walked past her mother on the way to the door. "Good night."

Letitia stared.

Clare stepped out into the hallway, more tired than she'd been earlier when she was only exhausted. Now her emotions were all out of whack. She wanted to defend Gage, no matter what his response to the offer of money to walk away had been.

Things with Gage had ended in a way they would never be put back together again, even if that was what she wanted. Selena was about to break up with Alex. Ember was about to marry Trey. Who knew how things would go with Gage? She had no clue if he would ever get to the place where he was interested in a relationship.

Rekindling what had burned hot once.

They were older, and hopefully wiser now. She knew he had a faith relationship with God, so he would follow all those rules she tried to avoid. Clare wanted the autonomy to make her own rules—live life the way she wanted, rather than what her mother dictated or what her failure took from her.

She blew out a breath, trying to push away all the angst while she checked with the nurse, then the officer on the door, then waited while the nurse asked Mrs. Mares if she was up to talking. No pressure, nothing official.

Clare glanced at the cop. "Did the SWAT lieutenant come by and interview her?"

"We got a statement when she was admitted. Hoping she'll say more tomorrow."

Clare nodded.

The nurse came back out and said, "She's awake, can't sleep actually. I think she'd like the company."

"Okay."

"No stress."

"I promise," Clare said.

She eased into the room and closed the door behind her. "Hi, I'm Clare Juarez. I run Vanguard Investigations. I'm helping the police with this case."

"As long as you're not one of those cops who arrested my husband just for trying to save me." Katrina Mares turned her head to look at the curtains that had been drawn closed over the window.

"Is it okay if I sit? I heard you can't sleep."

The woman shrugged one shoulder. Her blond hair had been washed and left to dry naturally, giving it a wave she probably paid to get straightened professionally. A bruise high on her cheekbone said she'd been struck. Her lip had been split, and defensive wounds covered her hands and arms.

"You fought him."

"Yes, I did." Katrina swallowed. "Not that it helped."

"At least you can say you tried."

Clare hadn't started doing that until she got out from under her mother's shadow and the army showed her how to grow a backbone. Since then she'd avoided her mother so she didn't slip back into that person who caved at everything. Who believed it was her fault bad things happened to her, and wished away the pain like it didn't matter.

She didn't ask Katrina to recount what'd happened to her. Instead, she asked, "Did the police show you photos to see if you can pick anyone out?"

Katrina shook her head. "They said they'd bring some in the morning."

If Clare could get a positive ID, Vanguard could get the cops an answer and save Katrina the pain of dragging it all out. They'd be one step closer by the time everyone woke up in the morning. She pulled out her phone. "I'm going to show you a group of photos. He might be in here, he might not. Either way, like fighting him, you can at least say you tried."

Her mother might be more results oriented, but Clare had to know for sure that she'd done everything she could. Not just that she took the easy route for the fastest win.

"How many of them were there?" Clare asked.

"Just one."

"Okay. Just let me know if you see him." Clare handed Katrina the phone and gave her a minute to swipe through the photos. She heard the intake of breath and turned back.

Katrina's face had paled. Her hand shook, holding the phone.

Clare waited.

"This is him." Katrina handed over the phone.

Clare looked at the photo, then turned it. "To confirm, this is the man you saw?"

Katrina nodded. "Yes."

"Thank you."

"He left me for dead."

"Tell me about him." She needed as much information as possible—and a face-to-face with the man the police had arrested. The police might not be worried about anything but bringing them all in. But what if there was more to it? What if this guy had something else planned? "Anything at all might help me figure out where to find him before he hurts someone else."

He might even plan to come after her, the way he'd targeted Alex.

Katrina said, "He's insane."

TWENTY-NINE

Gage ducked his head and let the rain fall on the back of his hood. The automatic doors ahead of him slid open, and he stepped inside, flicking the hood back and looking around. The lobby of Mountain Heights Retirement Home looked like a hotel, or a high-end apartment complex.

A couple in their forties walked out of a side door, holding hands.

Gage headed for the front desk, where a woman in scrubs sat at the computer. "Good evening."

She looked over. "Can I help you? Visiting hours are over shortly."

"I thought they were over at nine." It wasn't quite eight thirty. "I can be quick, if he wants to see me."

"Who are you wanting?"

Gage's stomach clenched. "Alistair McCauley."

She typed on her computer. "You're not on the normal list."

"This is..." He didn't even know how to describe it. "Can you just ask him if he's open to talking to me?" Gage flashed his badge. Even though he wore jeans and a dark red Henley, he wasn't above explaining who he was like this. "It's not official. It's personal."

"Pretty sure if he's awake, he'll want to talk to a brother in blue."

Gage tried to smile. His dad had been a cop? He hadn't had time to look into the old man's life. The first thing he'd learned was when he typed the address into his GPS and realized it was a retirement home. He didn't even know what the old man looked like.

"Wait here a moment." She got up and headed into a hallway.

Gage turned in the waiting area. The longer he was here, the greater the risk Dennis McCauley would show up. The last thing Gage needed was his half-brother and his boss discovering their personal connection. He didn't even know if he wanted to publicize it. First, he was going to tell Liam—if his sergeant hadn't already figured it out. When he'd met his father, he would decide the rest.

Part of him wanted to tell Clare.

Lord, I need Your help.

He had to let go of her, since it was so clear their lives didn't need to be intertwined. What had happened was in the past. No sense trying to resurrect what was dead, even if he was still attracted to her.

The truth was, Clare had built a life he respected. She was hardworking and a force for good in the world. If he wasn't a cop, he'd probably do exactly what she was doing. Or he'd be in her office first thing, asking for a job.

Wouldn't that be an awkward conversation.

When his phone buzzed with a notification, he realized he was smiling to himself like an idiot. He read the text from Liam.

CLARE SPOKE WITH KATRINA. VANGUARD HAS INFO WE DON'T.

Gage frowned and typed back,

IT'S NOT A COMPETITION.

They could ask Vanguard to share what they knew now, or wait until tomorrow morning and have an early-morning briefing. He asked Liam to send an email about a meeting at eight a.m.

"Mr. Deluca?"

He lowered the phone and stowed it. "Yep."

"Mr. McCauley is awake and would love a visitor." She turned for the hall, and he followed. "He took a nap earlier, so he's unable to sleep. Most of our residents turn in early, but some stay up later."

They passed a living room, expansive with a big TV on the wall playing a black-and-white show. Several older people were watching. Chatting. One guy was asleep with his feet up.

"This doesn't seem like a bad spot to end up in," Gage said.

She smiled. "You should see it in the summer. Those long evenings with plenty of sunlight until late. The patio is a social club, and we end up with a crowd asking for virgin daiquiris until eleven."

He chuckled. Then noticed he was at the door to a small apartment.

"I'll leave you to it." She wandered off, leaving him to face the open door.

He stared at it for a long moment, then pushed the door open all the way and stepped inside. An older African American man sat in an armchair beside a loveseat. The room had been decorated with a nod toward mountains and San Francisco's football team.

Gage smiled. "Shame about that last game."

The old man chuckled, and his whole torso moved with it. "That what you came here to talk about?" He eyed Gage. "You are...?"

He didn't come all the way in the room, but stood by the doorway when he said, "Renee Deluca's boy."

Alistair lifted a hand and waved him in. "Sit down, Son."

Gage's chest constricted like he'd put on Jasper's vest by mistake. He skirted the edge of the loveseat and sank into it. Alistair had a wide nose and darker brown eyes than Gage, who'd gotten a lot of his features from his mother. Dennis looked like his dad. "I'm Gage Deluca."

"Nice to meet you, Gage." Alistair might be in his eighties, but he seemed alert, even if his body didn't do what it might've once. "Renee's son?"

He nodded.

Alistair nodded and looked at his hands, clenched in his lap.

"I'm sorry to drop this on you, but I just found out."

Alistair must've been in his fifties, or late forties, at least when they'd gotten together. Gage's mom had died at fifty-seven. So Alistair had an affair with a woman thirty years younger than him. Not unheard of, but also not what Gage had been expecting.

"I never knew," Gage added.

But had Alistair known?

The old man wore a gold wedding band on his left hand. He'd had an affair, then. Gage was his dirty secret.

He looked around and spotted a framed photo on the fake fireplace. "You were a cop?"

"In Seattle," Alistair said. "Moved to Benson when the kids were teenagers, trying to give them a better life in a smaller city. A family-friendly environment."

"How did you meet Renee?"

"I arrested her." Alistair smoothed out an imaginary wrinkle over his knee. "She became an informant for me."

Gage winced. This type of thing was the reason why there were regulations about working with confidential informants, but maybe the rules had been more relaxed back then. "Who did she give you info on?"

"Local family. One of the brothers was making meth, and they were driving it over to Seattle for distribution." Alistair shook his head. "One of them decided to fill a truck and get it to Alaska. Your mom gave us the heads-up, and we stopped them before they hit the Canadian border."

"That's good." He never knew his mom had been a confidential informant for the police.

"She and I... It was a one-time thing. A mistake. I had a family, and when I broke it off"—the old man paused, tears glinting in his eyes—"I hurt her."

Gage couldn't speak past the lump in his throat.

"I always wondered."

He squeezed his eyes shut. The longing in his father's tone was the yearning he'd always had in his heart for his own child. The one he'd made with Clare. *A mistake.* But he'd never thought about it like that.

Now he knew it ended in tragedy. Loss.

His life had been this way because his mother made the choice to bury her hurt and tell him nothing.

"Thank you for seeing me," Gage managed to say. "I know you had no idea why I was here. I sprung this on you."

"I'm glad you did." Alistair nodded. "Now I know."

"Now you know what, Pops?" A woman strode in, carrying a stuffed tote bag. Fifties, dressed like she'd been at an office all day. Lines on her forehead as she glanced back and forth between them. "Who's your friend?" She dumped the bag on the kitchen counter and started unpacking groceries.

Alistair opened his mouth, then pursed his lips.

"Just a new friend," Gage said. "Do you need a hand with that?"

"No thanks...whoever you are."

If he told her his name, it might get back to McCauley. Then Gage would have to answer uncomfortable questions about why he was visiting the captain's father. Since he didn't know how Alistair felt about them all knowing, he kept his mouth shut.

"Someone who should be going, since visiting hours are almost over." Gage got up and went to stand in front of Alistair McCauley, then stuck his hand out. "It was very nice to meet you."

The old man clasped his hand and shifted to the edge of the seat.

Gage helped him get to his feet.

He pulled Gage close to his chest. Slapped him on the back—though there wasn't much strength to it.

Gage hugged his father for the first time.

"Very nice to meet you, Gage." The older man's voice was thick.

Gage swallowed back the emotion in his throat. "You too, sir."

"Come back soon." Alistair studied his face. "And get some sleep. You look tired."

THIRTY

C lare got out of the car and tried not to walk like she'd barely slept. It wasn't even six in the morning, but time would be limited for them to access this spot between PD detectives and further evidence collection. Follow-up look-arounds.

She stared at the laundromat, the front door slashed across with yellow police tape. "Wanna tell me why I'm at a crime scene at six in the morning?"

Peter winced. "I'd have brought you a cup of coffee, but..."

"This is a crime scene."

"Too right." Bob Davis, the head of her Cold Case department, sipped from a paper cup. "Wouldn't want to turn your stomach with all the blood."

Clare's eyebrows rose. "Instead of me asking what that means, why don't you fill me in while we go inside."

Peter nodded. "This way." He held a tablet under one arm and used a key to unlock the door. When the police taped up the crime scene, they'd also secured the entrances and exits so no one could sneak in. Like they were.

"Where'd you get the key?" she asked.

Bob coughed.

"Never mind." Clare sighed. "Tell me why I'm here."

"Right," Peter said. "The man Katrina Mares identified as her captor is Aaron Crenshaw."

Clare had received that name in her email, along with some basic information, last night just before midnight. Overnight, her people had done a full work-up on the guy and his entire life, then made a correlation to a crime at a laundromat for some reason. She'd tossed and turned all night, so she probably looked scary this morning. Barely presentable. Nothing like what her mother wanted her to be.

"And this?" she asked.

"Double homicide." Bob motioned to a door at the far end of the front of store where rows of state-of-the-art machines sat, quiet and unused. The whole place smelled like detergent and fabric softener.

"Ah." Clare glanced over at him as they walked. "The Estonians."

He nodded. "Guess we aren't going to get anything from them now."

She sighed. For weeks they'd been surveilling the owner of this place, or his family, trying to figure out their connection to a cold case Vanguard was currently working. A young girl who'd gone missing years ago. The family had zero evidence until someone had seen the girl in the background of a commercial for a check cashing joint.

That led them to the crime family who owned that business.

"They own this place, too?"

"Connected, yeah." Bob followed her, while she followed Peter.

The young man stopped in the hallway and looked at his tablet. His face had paled. He looked almost...

"In there?" Clare pointed at the open door, already spotting blood on the floor. When Peter nodded, she said, "Stay here."

Might not be his first crime scene, or his first dead body. But Clare didn't want Vanguard leaving evidence at a crime scene in the form of vomit—or anything else.

He nodded, a flash of relief in his eyes for a second.

She moved in front of him and looked at the office. Two desks, one facing her with the window behind it. One to the side, perpendicular. "The guy who runs it and the secretary."

"We can close our cold case." Bob's voice was low. "After I take the parents to the morgue to identify her."

"The secretary?" She wasn't going to assume and be wrong just because she didn't ask.

Bob nodded and stuck his hands in his pockets. "PD won't give me anything, but Peter here called and they sent over a copy of the photo. We were able to tell them who we believe she is. Parents confirmed when we went to their house and showed them. They need to make it formal though."

Clare didn't want to get sidetracked by how the former police officer, who'd served the time he'd been given for his crime, now found himself being treated by those who had been his brothers. Who believed he'd betrayed them and the badge. Never mind that Bob's daughter was an FBI agent in town, and his son-in-law-to-be was a Benson PD detective. "How long has the scene been here?"

"Day and a half."

"How did it get connected to Aaron Crenshaw?"

Peter said, "We have evidence that indicates the deceased male, Solomon Uzeska, is a known local forger. Driver's licenses, passports. Birth certificates. Basically anything you want, he can make it."

Bob entered the room, now wearing latex gloves. Carefully treading each footstep. The guy knew what to do at a crime scene, but she didn't envy him what would happen if the PD evidence techs collected proof he'd been here.

They'd likely arrest him on principle.

"Aaron is gonna run?" She wanted to know how he'd been aware to come here to get fake papers he could use to flee. But she had to tell the cops so they'd alert Homeland Security in case he fled the country. "Do we know he killed these two? Is that what we think?"

Peter, stood closer to her, nodded. "A payment was made from Crenshaw Industries to Solomon Uzeska's offshore accounts in Belize. Accounts we've been monitoring. His parents are in Italy, and they've been there more than two years without coming home. A proxy is running the company —into the ground, I might add—though no one seems to care."

"And Aaron?"

"Computer science major. He got into the company, and he's using that access and his skills to get new IDs."

Clare blew out a breath. "And he came here, picked up the stuff, and killed the two of them? Not a sustainable way to do business."

"Witnesses claim he came back here, and minutes later there were three shots. He didn't exit the way he came in, through the front. We've got surveillance of the street out back. Very grainy gray wash, so it's barely visible. He had on a hoodie, but we did the math, and the height and weight match Aaron."

"Okay," Clare said. "Where does he live?"

"I've got the address. But we still have one other to identify and locate."

"Looks like this one is the dangerous one. Even if it is a thin connection." They didn't know for sure if it was Aaron who'd killed these people, but the thread connecting them was good enough for her.

Bob called out from across the room, where he was rifling through a drawer of the file cabinet. "We could call in an anonymous tip to the PD. Tell them we heard screaming inside the house. Give his address."

Peter frowned. "It's his parents' house. Could be he's staying there."

"We can pass the information to the police department, and they can get a warrant. Or go question whoever is living there." Clare wasn't going to ruffle feathers.

It was her personal hangups that derailed her every time. Like a self-fulfilling prophecy of failure. With a situation this serious, she didn't want to risk another person being hurt. There had been too many injuries, and casualties, so far. The last thing she wanted was to lay her head down at night and feel the weight of responsibility for more than she'd already done.

"I already asked Lucas if it would hold weight, and he said it might be enough of a connection for a warrant."

"Good." Lucas was about to marry Peter's sister. Utilizing him as a resource within the PD was a good idea. "Let's send SWAT an email, tell them what we found."

Peter shifted his weight.

Clare glanced at the young man. "What is it?"

Bob came out of the office, tugging off his gloves. "My idea. That's what."

She frowned, about to ask what was going on, when someone said, "It's just after six. You all start work this early every day?"

She bit the inside of her lip and turned.

Gage strode down the hall wearing his uniform pants, shirt, and boots. Jacket. Stuff he'd wear around the office rather than the vest and helmet he added for a callout. Of course he looked well rested. Like he'd slept ten hours and had a good breakfast. She'd inhaled a granola bar on the way out the door and washed it down with coffee in the car.

"Morning." Bob rocked back and forth on his shoes.

"Yes, it is." Gage paused. "I was thinking eight a.m. briefing. Not a six o'clock meeting at a crime scene."

Clare didn't want to have to explain everything Peter had just told her. But if he didn't know already, how had he come to be here? She glanced at her young employee.

"I already called SWAT," Peter said. "Let them know what we've got."

"Right." Clare didn't know what to do with that.

"Bob and I will be outside." Peter nodded to the older man and tipped his head, then the two of them strode out.

Behind Gage's back, Bob gave her two thumbs-ups.

Clare bit down on her molars.

"Everything okay?" Gage asked.

Great. She must've looked unhinged as well as exhausted. "I had a heart to heart with my mom last night. Then I talked to Katrina Mares, since I was in the hospital anyway. She agreed and was able to ID the man who held her." She just hadn't been able to pinpoint where she'd been. Aside from the fact it'd been a back room. Drywall and mud. No light fixture, just wires. Lights on stands blinding her.

Katrina had been beaten and tied to a chair and held for hours before she was left for dead in the park by Steven Phoenix.

Gage nodded. "I know your people believe Aaron Crenshaw is connected to this crime. I called the detectives, and he's going to call Bob. A breakfast meeting with them so they can go over it all. Make some progress on the case."

"Oh. Great." She had to say, "Bob doesn't usually get

much more than basic politeness, and sometimes even that seems like a stretch."

Gage started to speak but caught himself. "I'd like to get to know the man he is now. Not the guy everyone says he used to be."

When he looked at her like that, it made her wish he would do the same with her.

Could she actually hope for that?

Clare wanted to believe.

THIRTY-ONE

"Let's go outside." Gage motioned to the front of the building. "It's pretty ripe in here."

Clare nodded. Her face was as pale as the walls, her black hair making her skin seem even lighter than normal. She had dark circles around her eyes.

He wondered if he was the one who put them there.

"Are you feeling okay?" he asked, then stopped her in the front room of the store. "One sec before we go out. I'm..." He held up his hand, trying to figure out how to say this. "I'm sorry."

That was probably the simplest—and best.

Clare's eyes widened.

"If you're really so surprised that I would apologize to you, then I've got more to do to repair this relationship than I thought." He winced. "Okay, so it's not exactly a relationship but..."

"It's not nothing," she said, a guarded expression on her face. "Or just colleagues. Not with our history."

He nodded. "Now that I'm supposed to be living what I said I believed, that Jesus took my sin, I'm supposed to apologize and ask for forgiveness." He took a breath. "I shouldn't have yelled at you last time I saw you. People were hurt. Dakota caused all that damage and put lives at risk. I was mad at him, and that spilled out into being mad at you, and I'm sorry."

"Thank you." She put her hand on his shoulder, leaned up, and touched her lips to his cheek.

Gage blushed. He ducked his head. "Can we talk about something later?"

"About us? Or the case?"

"Actually, neither." He found himself saying, "But there's no one else I want to talk about it with than you."

Maybe she was a safe bet because she wasn't part of his life all the time, or for the foreseeable future. They could part ways again, similarly to how they had before. She might get the contract with Benson PD for her company, then make sure she never had to work with him again.

Or he just wanted to tell her because she was the person who meant the most to him in his life that still lived, even if that was a long time ago. His mom was gone. His dad was who he wanted to talk to her about.

Who else did that leave?

He was going to tell Liam pretty soon, but for some reason he wanted to tell Clare first. She of all people would understand what it meant to him to finally know who his father was. They'd talked about their dads a lot at one point.

But they also needed to work right now. "Breakfast? I'll get SWAT to meet us there. We can compare notes while one of my guys waits for the judge to get into work this morning so he can get a signed warrant for Aaron's house."

She eyed him. "They did fill you in, didn't they?"

"Hungry?"

Clare blew out a breath. "Not exactly, but breakfast is probably a good idea."

She drove behind him, and when they were seated at a circular booth big enough for eight, she slid in beside him. Gage didn't like being boxed in but got to turn and face her. "The guys aren't here, so..."

He took a breath while she studied him with a soft expression. Gage put his arm up on the back of the seat. "I met my father yesterday."

She gasped.

He told her about finding his birth certificate—a different copy from what he had—in his mom's things, and how he'd found the old man's name. Then his address. "I went to see him. Alistair McCauley."

"As in...Captain McCauley?" Her eyes widened.

"Dennis is, I guess, my half-brother." He could hardly believe it. "He doesn't know. I haven't decided how far I'll go announcing my father's sins to anyone it concerns. But I saw him. He knows who I am. Alistair."

She gave him a small smile, lifted her hand, and touched his cheek. "That's wonderful, Gage."

He nodded. "God gave me a gift I never would have had."

Someone cleared their throat.

"Don't mind us." Liam slid into the other end of the bench, smirking. Blake pulled out a chair. Peter and Bob were two tables away, drinking from white stone mugs and waiting for the detective.

Jasper sat down on the other side of Clare. "Good morning."

"Morning, guys." She smiled.

They all stared at her, captivated.

Gage said, "Okay, coffee and down to business."

Ten minutes later he swallowed his first bite of hashbrowns—officially making all right in the world—and said, "Anything from Steven Phoenix overnight?"

Blake nodded. "Third shift sergeant had him in the box for two hours. Steven gave up his real last name, and we confirmed his online persona. He did good keeping it all disconnected. Gave us the runaround."

"Vanguard would have found out soon enough," Clare said.

Everyone paused what they were doing. More than one mug stopped before lips. They all stared at her.

"I'm just saying," she added.

Liam snorted. Blake actually grinned. Gage said, "So would the PD."

"Yeah, but Vanguard would've been faster." She grinned and took a sip of coffee.

Gage was pretty sure they'd have looked better doing it, but no way he was going to say that to her. Not in front of the guys. "And we have Aaron's name." He turned to Clare. "What about what Katrina told you?"

She nodded, setting her cup down. "That Aaron is insane? She has no idea what—if anything—he has planned. Just that he beat her and tied her to a chair. She didn't see anyone else. She might be able to confirm it's the place she was held after we find it, but she can't tell us where it is."

Jasper grunted and took another bite of his omelet.

"Until Alex wakes up, we're at the end of intel we're able to gather without pressuring everyone we've already talked to again." Clare paused. "Or talking to my mother."

Gage didn't want to go there.

Clare glanced at him. "She confirmed she offered you money to break up with me, by the way."

The guys stilled again.

"Planning on giving away all our secrets today?" He didn't think she'd mention the baby, but she'd told them enough.

Clare shrugged. "I guess she thought in her twisted way of thinking that she was doing me a favor. Because if you'd taken the money, then she'd have been right about you."

"I didn't."

"So she got you to walk away, and she saved the money."

"Did she spend it on you?"

"She probably just used it to buy another pair of shoes." Clare made a face and drank some more coffee. She hadn't touched her eggs, but she'd plowed through most of the serving of potatoes she'd drowned in both ketchup and mayonnaise. "Since you apologized, I figure you should know it didn't come from me. That was all Mom."

He wanted to ask her how she'd been, but his phone rang and he didn't want to have that part of the conversation in front of three cops under him. He looked at the screen. "Warrant is signed."

The boys all got up. Everyone tossed cash on the table, and they headed out. Four uniformed SWAT officers and Clare.

Six minutes later, they were suited up and in position outside the residence.

"You're a man down, right?" Clare came over from her car, securing a bulletproof vest over her wool sweater.

He didn't like this, and tried to figure out how to tell her no.

Liam slapped his shoulder. "Yep. Fall in, Ms. Juarez. You're with the lieutenant on the front door. Blake. Jas. You take the back. I've got the side door by the garage."

They all called out confirmation. Checked the radio. Got in position.

Gage looked at Clare. "I don't like you being—"

She pointed at the corner of the porch, under the roof overhang. "Cameras."

Gage looked where she'd pointed and frowned.

Every nerve ending he had went on alert. He heard the distant, muffled ratchet of a shotgun.

Clare turned toward him, already moving. He tackled her, and they both went down.

The front door exploded above their heads.

THIRTY-TWO

Clare's head glanced off the front step. She hissed. "Ow."

Gage started to shift off her.

Clare caught movement in the doorway. She reached across his back, grasped his vest under his left arm, and rolled him to the side as she turned onto her left hip. She lifted her gun at the same time and squeezed off two shots.

A muffled yell came from inside, and the door slammed.

She heard footsteps from beyond the front door grow quieter. "He ran off."

Gage grunted, then pushed off the ground, held his hand out, and helped her to her feet. Much like when he'd apologized she couldn't quite believe what she was seeing—or hearing. The man Gage had turned to was amazing. A good guy, nothing like who she thought he had been when he left her, alone and pregnant.

She thought he'd been living the high life.

Instead, he'd become a cop. Found faith in Jesus Christ, just like her friend Ember. Now he was a SWAT lieutenant. Someone he could be proud of.

And still, on top of all that, he'd found his father after all this time.

Why did that seem so much more important than her making a success out of Vanguard?

Everything in her wanted to get lost in how amazing he was, and how confusing the whole situation with him turned out to be, but there was a gunman to find.

She stepped past him. "Let's go."

One of his guys raced around the corner of the house, drawn by the shots.

Gage said, "Copy that." He touched her shoulder. "I go first."

She caught the expression on his face. "Copy that."

Blake followed her, Gage went first, and they headed into the house. The gunman— possibly Aaron, but she didn't know for sure even if this was his parents' house—had fled into the house after he blew a hole in the door.

Gage pushed splintered sections of the door out of the way. He moved down the hall with his knees slightly bent. She could easily get distracted by the line of his back, and the display of strength. He held his gun up, shifting it as he turned each direction.

They covered each other, and Blake backed them both up.

Entryway. Front room, no TV—just a pool table and a couple of brown leather recliners. Empty bottles and glasses littered the surfaces. Books had been pulled from shelves and tossed on the floor, but it seemed more like hard living than a break-in.

The kitchen smelled like old pizza. Dishes spilled out of the sink, and the dishwasher stood with the door open, ready to catch some unsuspecting person in the shins.

Clare had done that before.

"Clear." She checked the pantry. "Clear. What about the

garage?" They hadn't had an extra earpiece, so she couldn't hear what they all had going on over comms.

"Liam is cutting him off, disabling any vehicles so he can't get out that way."

She glanced back at Blake. "Good thinking."

There was something about Blake she couldn't put her finger on. He lived behind a thick wall of self-protection, and it made her want to dig down to see what was below the surface. Problem was, that wall had a giant KEEP OUT sign tacked onto it. One day a woman would crack the wall and get inside. Clare wasn't sure she wanted to witness the fallout when that happened.

All Gage's friends were great. Even Dakota, though it'd been clear he had issues. They'd mentioned at breakfast he'd been put on a two-week suspension, so they were a man down. No one had said why, but she wasn't sure it was about the van plowing into that department store. At least, not completely.

They continued down the hall to a wider living area. Huge dining table, chairs askew. A cobweb glinted in the light from the patio, a strand that connected the chandelier light fixture to the ceiling.

It bobbed with a breeze of air.

Clare spun.

"Hands up!" Gage approached a young woman, lowering his weapon as he went. She wore a bikini so there were definitely no weapons hidden anywhere.

She stopped halfway in the back door, a friend right behind her.

The friend started to turn.

"Nope!" Clare moved around Gage and grabbed the first one's wrist. "Go take a seat on the couch." She dragged the friend inside also and tugged her the same direction. "Where is he?"

"We were in the hot tub. We don't know anything!"

Blake stood off to the side, where he folded his arms. "Then where are your towels?" They weren't exactly dripping on the couch. "Tell us where Aaron is, and *no lying.*"

Clare wandered the room. She wanted to be aware if anyone came in, and she had to defend the two cops in the room from an armed man. One Katrina had described as *insane.* They needed to search the rest of the house.

"Blake, stay here." Gage crossed the room. "They don't leave. Call in backup and get them dressed and at the station for questioning."

"I'm not sayin' nothin'!" one of them wailed. "I know my rights!"

"Good." Clare spoke over her shoulder. "You *should* know your rights."

Gage chuckled under his breath. "Come on. We need to search the east side. Jasper found a locked door, so he's working on that and Liam is scouting outside. We think there are cameras, so if we can find where the surveillance feed goes to, then we can see where he went."

The idea this guy was hiding somewhere wasn't good.

They walked through a media room. Then a home gym. Upstairs had a wide window, with a view of the pool. Debris floated on the surface. Clothing. A chip bag, and several empty cans.

Clare wrinkled her nose.

"Don't like the house?" He spoke to her, but kept his attention on the house and finding the guy who nearly killed them. "You grew up in one not much different from this."

"Two streets over. And it wasn't this big."

"Bigger than my trailer."

"You know, no one else has an issue with where you came from. Except you." He'd always had a complex about being the guy from the wrong side of the tracks.

"People say stuff. Rub it in to make themselves feel better," he said. "Mostly my mom. Wanting to make sure I never forgot who we were."

"I say who I am," Clare said. "Not someone else."

"So who are you?"

"A soldier and a small business owner."

"What were you saying about being more than I thought I was?" Gage didn't finish the thought.

There was no time to ask him to elaborate, either.

She heard a rustle behind her and spun around, gun up. Empty hall. "This way."

Gage followed her into a huge bedroom, rumpled covers. The curtain ruffled, and she headed for it walking slowly. Making almost no sound while her mind spun on what he'd said. She missed this. Gun up, tracking a suspect. She'd never been a cop, but she'd done this kind of stuff in the army. On operations where they'd teamed up with the CIA, usually Ember which was how they'd met.

Adrenaline-laced blood coursed through her body. Energizing her and pumping fresh oxygen to her brain. She was alive when she did this kind of work. More alive than sitting at a desk doing paperwork, or even leading a meeting.

She stood to one side and whipped the curtain back.

A black cat let out a screech of protest.

"Sorry." Clare let the curtain move back into place.

As it moved, she caught a shift in the corner of her eye. Emerging from the closet.

She raced to the door and slammed him between the door and the frame. He cried out. She hauled the door open, and he stumbled.

Clare slammed her gun hand down on his forearm. He dropped the shotgun, and she kicked him in the stomach. He fell to the floor.

Clare stuck her weapon back in its holster and rolled the guy to his front, knelt, and tugged his arms behind his back while he squirmed. "Cut it out." She clasped his wrists so he couldn't go anywhere and looked up.

Liam stood at the door. Gage closer to her, covering her with his weapon.

"I need cuffs," she said over her shoulder.

"She needs an application. Maybe we should ask Russ if he'd hire her for SWAT."

A slight pull tugged up Gage's lips. "I don't think she wants to share a locker room with you." He slid out cuffs and held them out. "Here you go, hero. But I can't let you read him his rights."

THIRTY-THREE

C lare hauled up the suspect to his feet, hands cuffed behind his back. "I'm not really looking for a job."

Gage figured from her face that she knew he was aware. Still, he said, "I know." Mostly so Liam would get off this train. "Sergeant O'Connell, take this man to the living room. He's under arrest for attempted murder of a police officer."

"Yes, Lieutenant." Liam took the cuffed man's elbow and led him from the room.

"That isn't the guy we came here to find. He could just be a squatter." Clare kept talking while he crossed to her. "For all we know, he isn't one of them."

Gage tugged her in for a hug and wrapped his arms around her. Clare stiffened for a second, then sighed and wrapped her arms around him. "We make a pretty good team."

"We always did," she said. "That was never the problem."

He leaned back. "You're pretty amazing, and if you were a cop, I would force the paperwork through to get you transferred to my team."

"If I was a cop—" She grinned. "Let's face it. I'd be *leading* your team."

Gage snorted. He wasn't going to tell her, but she was probably right. The kind of woman Clare was, she'd probably be his superior. "You'd make all our lives miserable."

She chuckled. "But I'd get results."

He grinned. Having her in his arms, feeling the warmth of her up against him. He hadn't been a Christian for long, but all those good ideals and principals for living seemed to fade from his mind along with Paul's words about being single.

He'd been content. But now she was back in his life, he was rethinking his ideas. And maybe that was the whole point. He'd been focused.

Now he was focused on *her*.

He leaned down, realizing kissing sounded like an excellent idea he hadn't had in a long time. He knew the truth of what they'd both lost. He'd found his father. The issues between him and Clare had come out, so now they could start to do the work of seeing if there was still something there.

Only, he already knew that answer, didn't he?

Gage's lips touched hers. The briefest of kisses. Adrenaline, good sense out the window—if this was even a bad idea, which he wasn't sure was true.

Clare's arms tightened around him, and she tucked her body closer to his.

It was familiar and new at the same time. Everything he'd had and wanted for his future. Someone to be close to, who loved him regardless of all the ways he didn't measure up. Someone he could show the same love to.

His earpiece crackled in his ear. "Lieutenant." It was Jasper. "I found something you're gonna wanna see."

Gage pulled his lips back from Clare's and said, "I doubt it."

She frowned. "What?"

He shifted so she'd know he wasn't talking to her and said, "What is it, Hollingsworth?" Gage didn't want to let Clare go. Not yet.

She stayed tucked up against him, so he pressed a kiss to her forehead. Both of them were sweaty in their rumpled protective gear, but it was a sweet moment anyway. A stolen minute of togetherness he'd missed.

Jasper said, "East side of the house. Second floor."

"On our way." Gage stepped back from Clare and immediately realized two things. He didn't like being far from her, and the need to be close could get dangerous. If they were going to build something, it would end with an aisle and her wearing a ring. Not out of order like it would have been last time.

She didn't say anything as they left the room and he tried to figure out which side of the house was east. Gage glanced back and saw the pink on her cheeks. She bit her lip.

He looked back where he was going so he didn't trip over something. "So that wasn't the guy we were looking for, Aaron Crenshaw."

"That's what I was saying."

Before he'd kissed her. "But you're right, I don't think it's a squatter. I think he's one of our bank robbery suspects. Hopefully this one will talk."

"One more to find, and we're done, right?"

Gage stopped at an open door. "Done?"

"With me working with you on this case. Because Russ told us to." She frowned, but it seemed more like she was trying to figure out what to say. "Which means I can hopefully sign a contract with the PD and get Vanguard signed on as a consultant."

"Okay." What was she saying?

"Maybe after that, things could go back to just being personal between us. Not work."

Gage nodded.

"Unless you want to write me a recommendation letter that Russ can take into account. About how amazing Vanguard is, and how instrumental we were in bringing this crew of suspects in." She smiled.

He didn't like the note of irritation that sprung up in him then. As if she'd only been hanging around to prove herself. Peter was the one who'd called him to the homicide scene, not Clare. She might not even have contacted him at all.

He turned away. "We'll see."

"What—"

Jasper stepped into the doorway.

"What have you got?" Gage moved into the room, Clare behind him. Though he heard something whispered low between them, Gage ignored it and took in what he was looking at. A bland room where the drywall had been mudded but no primer or paint. If it wasn't the second floor, he would think it was an unfinished basement.

In the center was a single wood chair that matched the dining table chairs downstairs. Four lights on stands marked corners of a square around the chair.

"This is where Katrina was held."

He turned back to Clare. "You're sure?"

"We could show her photos to confirm, but this is exactly what she described. They put a hood over her head and led her in bound so she had no idea where she was."

The one guy they still had to find had done this.

Gage said to Jasper. "We need to know if the guy we just arrested knew what was going on here."

Jasper stepped into the hall and got on the radio. Gage

heard the exchange in his earpiece and looked back at the room.

"All so he could get the doctor to kill Alex—or try to." Clare wandered the room. "What's in there?"

The door at the far end looked like any home interior door. "Let's find out." Gage strode over, lifted his boot, and kicked the door open. Even if it might not have been locked, it was still satisfying to do that. More than turning a handle.

Clare stepped in first. "Whoa."

At the center stood a folding plastic table with stuff bundled on it. Clothes and rope. A duffel, and a pair of black tactical boots. Papers lined the walls—huge blueprints and schematics. Computer systems. A building had been taken apart and drawn out in plans, layer by layer. Rooms. Electronic access ports.

"What is this place?" Gage wondered aloud. Maybe it was this guy's next target. He turned to Clare because she hadn't said anything.

Her face had paled. Her hand shaky when she lifted it and pointed. "This is Vanguard. All of it. This is *my* building."

Gage took a step toward her. "Clare—"

She pulled out a phone and made a call. "Four-seven-two-nine. Code Black."

He heard a distant voice say, "Understood."

Clare hung up the phone and made another call. She put it to her ear. "I know. I need your help, but you need to leave the baby with a sitter." She rattled off the address where they were, then hung up.

Blew out a breath.

We're gonna find him.

We don't know what he has planned.

He could've said either, but the words didn't come. Gage

opened his arms so he could give her another hug. What else could he do? She needed comfort. Someone to stand beside her in the unknown. The worry of what might happen.

At least she didn't run for the door.

Clare shook her head. "Later. Find something that says what his plan is."

Guess it's time to work. He studied her for a second, noting how hard it was for her to pull herself together. But she did it.

God, help us.

THIRTY-FOUR

Clare wanted nothing more than to step into his arms, or let him take over and solve this problem for her. But it was *her* business. Her people, her friends and family. But she couldn't.

Leaning on Gage would lead to letting him take the work of fixing her problems, and that wasn't the woman she ever wanted to be.

Clare steeled herself against the freak out that boiled in her stomach. She bit down on her back teeth and tried to assess the stuff all over the walls like it wasn't her livelihood. Her people. Someone was targeting the thing she held most dear. She would lose everything again and she'd barely survived last time.

Clare sucked in a breath, like she was trying not to cry— maybe she was.

Commotion kicked off by the door.

She turned to see Liam shove the guy she'd cuffed into the room. "This?"

The guy sputtered. "What..?" He looked around. "I've never been in here!"

Clare tried to get a read on whether that was the truth or not. "A woman was kidnapped the other day. She was held in that room." Clare pointed over his shoulder. "You're telling me you had no clue?"

He shrugged his shoulders, but it was difficult to do so with his hands cuffed behind his back. "I had no idea Berlin was into this."

"Phoenix. Berlin." Gage shot them a look. "Those are your real names?"

Clare figured the laundromat forgers might've made more than Aaron's new IDs—before being shot.

"His name is Berlin."

"And the rest of you?" Liam asked.

"London was in the van when it went over the cliff."

Gage said, "So he's the one you all murdered. Why?"

The guy lifted his chin, indicating Clare. "For talking too much to her. He was gonna give us away."

Gage turned to Clare. She told him, "At the bank, during the robbery." To the kid, she said, "Who killed the teller?"

"Berlin, of course. Miami was with him. I didn't even see it." He shifted his feet, desperation lacing his tone.

"Who is Miami?"

Disgust washed over his expression. "That traitor. Berlin said he was gonna take care of him."

Gage looked at her. Clare mouthed *Alex,* and he nodded.

Liam tugged on the guy's elbow. "What else did Berlin say?"

The guy tried to act like he had no idea. Clare wasn't going to let her livelihood and the lives of people she knew hang on one uncooperative witness. "You ever heard the name Vanguard?"

"What's that mean?"

"It's someone who stands out in front of other people. Like a first line of defense."

"Sure. I got a shooter game I play like that." He made a face. "Whatever."

"What about these maps and plans?" She waved at the wall closest to her.

"I told you I ain't never been in here." He almost wailed the words.

"Behind you." Peter squeezed around Liam and the cuffed man. "Almost got them all. It's a shame."

Gage said, "Excuse me?"

Clare turned to survey the photos, leaving the cops in the room to deal with their suspect while she looked more at the blueprints.

"I wanted to go undercover. Try to get in on the crew." Peter breezed in and set down his laptop. "Bob's been talking about operations where he went undercover."

"There's a training course you have to go on first," Gage pointed out.

Peter moved next to his shoulder and breathed the word, "Chevalier."

"Yes." Clare chuckled. "The undercover training course is with Chevalier in Last Chance County."

Gage shook his head. "Why does that scare me, and I literally have no idea what you guys are talking about?"

Liam murmured his agreement. "I'll get this guy back downstairs. Since he's apparently useless."

The young man sputtered, but the noise dispersed.

Clare turned to Peter, who hadn't moved. "Let's figure this out. But as soon as I'm back at my desk, I'll put in the request."

If she hadn't been standing in front of him, the kid would've probably jumped up and down, pumping his fist in the air. Done some kind of twenty-two-year-old male version of a happy dance.

"So tell me what this is." She tried to find the code at the bottom that would tell her what version this was. They'd gone through so many when she moved the company from a store front downtown out to the office building they now occupied. "Other than our building."

Peter squeezed her shoulder. "Building plans." He walked a circuit around the room. "Electronic schematics. The entire breakdown of our computer network. Except for..."

"Yep." She didn't look at Gage. If she explained, it would be *after* he signed a nondisclosure. "What else?"

"Entrances and exits."

"But not security codes."

"No, he has how it's wired up, but not how to disable. Or the override that, of course, I know nothing about."

Clare would've laughed at any other time. "You, or Simon?" His twin brother had settled in the tech department, where Peter wanted to be undercover and all the other stuff that came with it.

"Both, actually."

"Bet?"

Peter grinned.

"Maybe you and your twin should bet each other that you can't find this Berlin guy before the police do." Working together had to be better than competing. They should pool their resources, even if it was to get one up on the police.

A result was a result.

"Aaron Crenshaw?" When Gage nodded, Peter continued, "Sie is already on it." His gaze slid to her. "Using the thing that lets us see the stuff."

"Right." Gage folded his arms. "All your supersecret spy

stuff is going to find this guy, and hopefully save any lives that are in danger."

"I want to say it doesn't matter if the building blows up." Clare sighed. "I really want to say it's just a building, and that people's lives matter far more. Which they do. And it's why I had them all clear out to a safe location. But really, it's *my* building."

Gage set his hand on her shoulder and gave it a squeeze. "So what's his plan? And where do we find him?"

"Maybe I can help with that."

Clare spun at that voice. They swept toward each other, and she gave Ember a hug. "Thanks for coming."

"You need all hands on deck, so I..." Ember paused. "Oh...huh."

"Not quite my reaction, but not far from it."

"You go get coffee. Gage can rattle that guy downstairs' cage, and I'll figure this out."

Gage glanced between her and Ember. Clare said, "This is my friend Ember."

He stepped forward, his hand out. "I know Trey."

"And you and Clare were high school sweethearts? I might be a stay-at-home mom right now, but Clare and I worked covert ops together. If you have questions, you should know it's classified. But I can kill you with just my thumb. *Especially* if you hurt her."

Clare chuckled. It was like a release valve unclogged, and she found herself bent forward, both hands on her knees.

Peter said, "She's lost it."

"I've never seen her laugh like that."

Gage's boots appeared beside hers, and he rubbed a hand up and down her back. "I have." She straightened, and he dropped his hand.

Clare caught it. "Let's go talk to him again. Maybe he's

remembered something." They headed out still holding hands, leaving her friend and her employee with their mouths open. She called back, "Get to work!"

Peter yelled, "Yes, ma'am!"

Clare swiped under her eye.

Gage squeezed her hand. "They love you."

"Yeah, they do." Clare had to say, "I used to get mad that they treated me like their CEO. Not Ember, she's a friend and not on the payroll right now. My employees, though? I wanted to be their buddy. Their teammate. They acted like I was their boss. But you're right. Because it's both."

"I've been wanting the guys on SWAT to treat me like their lieutenant when I've been one of them for years." He paused at the top of the stairs. "It's happening, just slowly. The shift in who I am and who they are."

"Like you're all growing."

He nodded. As soon as he stepped down, her phone started to ring. Clare pulled it out and saw her mother's number. She swiped the screen. "Yeah, Mom. What's up?"

A hiss of breath crackled the speaker. That was odd. She presumed her mother was at the hospital with Selena, watching over Alex while the doctors got him to wake up. Maybe he was awake now and talking, giving them information she could sorely use. Alex might even know where to find Aaron Crenshaw.

"Mom." She needed her to talk. "Mom."

Gage turned on the stairs.

"He...here," Letitia began, barely audible over the voices in the background. Hospital staff?

"Mom, what happened?" Cold threaded through Clare's veins.

"He hit me. He took Selena."

THIRTY-FIVE

S elena's head pounded. She opened her eyes again, but it was still pitch-black. So black she couldn't see her hands when she lifted them in front of her face. Though she could feel the zip ties cutting into her skin, she'd made sure she had space between her hands when he tightened them.

Thank you, Clare.

She needed to tell her mom's commanding officer exactly that the second she saw her.

Which she would. Selena was going to get out of this because Clare had taught her what to do.

She had to be in the trunk of a car because she felt the rumble of the road under her hip. Scratchy carpet. Enough room to move but not much more than that. Loud rock and roll music blaring—and not the good kind.

She got her knee up to her middle and brought her bound hands down. Hard. Pain sliced through her wrists where the ties dug in, but she felt the snap and her hands were free.

The car swerved around a corner.

Selena rolled and came up against the side wall, also carpeted.

He slowed the car. She knew it was a him, because she'd seen his face when he hit Letitia over the head. Selena had been distracted from what was happening to Alex because Clare's mom had been telling her stories of Clare in preschool and elementary. Funny jokes she used to tell.

Recalling them now made it so the reality of her situation dissipated a little.

Enough she didn't realize until the car fully stopped that he'd parked. The engine shut off. Then the music. A door slammed.

The trunk of the car flipped up, and blinding light shined on her face. She kept her fingers linked so it looked like she was still tied up, gasping even though she didn't want to.

Clare's coaching filled her mind. The sound of her voice, calm in Selena's ear.

"Where are my diamonds?"

Selena blinked.

"Alex took my diamonds. Where are they?" Her abductor grabbed her jacket and hauled her up.

She sucked in a breath through her nose. "Alex...what?"

"My. Diamonds." He breathed in her face, his gray eyes freaky. Dead almost. "Or are you as dumb as you look."

You have no idea who or what I am. He probably figured she was some bimbo, just arm candy for Alex and his social-media-famous life.

He pulled her out of the car. She didn't get her feet down before he shoved her. Selena fell to the ground, and he kicked her. Again and again. Her shoulder. Her hip. Her midsection. She couldn't hold it back any longer and cried out.

He laughed. "Tell me where the diamonds are. He stole them from me, then went to you. Where did you go?"

She tried to think. They'd gone to the park and met with Clare. That was where Alex had been shot. The diamonds? The only place Alex had been separated from her was when he'd asked to use the bathroom. They'd gone to Vanguard before the park because Clare hadn't been at the office.

"Talk!" Spit landed on her cheek.

"Vanguard."

Aaron Crenshaw stared at her. "What did you just say?"

THIRTY-SIX

Gage stepped off the elevator, Clare right beside him. A group of cops hung in the hall, looking worried. Far more commotion than normal but what he'd expect after an armed man barged into the hospital and kidnapped a woman.

"What happened?" Gage called out the question to no one in particular.

One of the on-duty officers met him halfway, a glassy expression on his face. Blood smudged on his sleeves and neck. He'd held someone that was injured.

"Were you here?" Gage asked him.

He nodded. "My partner stepped in. He stabbed her, hit the lawyer on the head, and took the girl. I was in the restroom."

Gage clapped him on the shoulder. Not because the guy hadn't made a mistake, but more because he had enough guilt over it on him already. Gage knew how that felt. "Did she…"

"She's in surgery." The guy looked at his hands, then backed up again. "They're saying she should pull through, but it's touch and go right now. Her husband came over with the kids." He motioned behind him, but Gage couldn't see with the crowd of cops in the hall.

A nurse wound between two officers and smiled at something someone said.

Clare shifted beside Gage. "And my mom?"

"Being checked out over there." The officer motioned to a room.

"Thanks." Clare looked at him. "I'll get her to ID who it was."

Gage said to the cop, "I'm glad there's a chance she'll pull through. I'll be praying."

He nodded. "Thanks, Lieutenant."

Gage backed off down the hall, needing to be alone for a moment. He didn't like feeling powerless. Surrendering his life to God meant giving up the need to control everything, but that didn't mean the dislike of feeling like he had no control had gone. Maybe it would never go away. Or he was supposed to practice that surrender every day. Every moment.

He found an alcove past the vending machine, leaned back against the wall, and closed his eyes. Took a few moments to pray for the injured officer and her family. For Letitia, even if he cared less about her than a cop. He shouldn't, so he practiced that as well. But the cop's situation was far more precarious than hers right now.

He prayed for Selena, a sweet young woman who'd stood up to him when he confronted Clare about Selena being their daughter.

Gage prayed that strength he'd seen meant she could withstand whatever was happening to her right now.

Then he called his suspended teammate and let it ring till the call went to voicemail.

Gage hung his head. "Dakota, it's me. I just wanna know

you're..." *Not spiraling.* "...all right. Call me back." He ended the call and let out a long breath, praying then for his friend.

"There you are, Lieutenant."

Gage opened his eyes as Captain McCauley headed toward him. He pushed off the wall. "Did you need something, Cap?"

"We'll get to that."

Gage frowned.

"First update me on what your team is doing."

"Right. The guys are interrogating everyone we have in lockup to find out where Aaron might have gone and what his plan might be. Clare Juarez is confirming the suspect's ID with her mom." Gage squeezed the back of his neck. "We have no idea why he might be targeting Vanguard or what connection he has to them."

That part made no sense.

Aaron had taken Selena for the diamonds, but why already have a schematic of Vanguard? Unless he had a plan involving their building. How could there be a connection between the two things?

Gage continued, "Vanguard is looking for any property Aaron Crenshaw owns, in case he took her there. All associates and their addresses. Family. Friends. A childhood favorite spot to go. Anything the company owns. Buildings. A place he might've spent time or somewhere he'd know is abandoned. They evacuated their building, but they're watching in case he shows up there." He added, "Priority is finding Selena and capturing the suspect."

McCauley nodded. "Agreed."

Gage tried to focus, but he was also trying to see a familial similarity between the two of them. The fact they were half-brothers might change nothing about their relationship. They might only ever be two cops who knew each other at work.

No more.

"And now the other reason I was looking for you."

Gage froze. The look on the captain's face was...

"Our other business. Where you went looking for my father, and he won't say why you were there talking to him. My sister had to tell me he had a visitor she's never seen before."

Gage wasn't going to lie, but he also didn't know how to explain it without Dennis finding out they were brothers.

"You never served together when my dad was a cop. He's been retired longer than that." McCauley folded his arms, stretching the sleeves of his uniform jacket. "How do you know him?"

"I don't, really," Gage said. "That was the first time we'd ever met."

"Why were you there?"

"Honestly? It's not really your business." Gage knew the captain wouldn't like it, but until he'd figured this out, it was all he had.

McCauley got in his face. "Tell me what you wanted with my dad."

"Nothing. I just stopped by to tell him who I am."

"And why would he care?"

Gage winced. "It's complicated."

McCauley pressed his lips together. "I bet it is."

"Excuse me?" Gage had been feeling powerless over Selena's kidnapping. This feeling wasn't too different, except no one had been kidnapped. The circumstances weren't any of his doing—or his fault. Yet here he was, dealing with the aftermath of it. "Look," he began, trying to be diplomatic. "When there's something to talk about, we can talk about it. Right now there's a case to work, and I need to focus on finding a missing young woman."

McCauley opened his mouth to say something.

"Gage?" Clare stepped into sight at the end of the hall.

He could've kissed her again right then, but not in front of a superior. Instead, he said, "Excuse me, Captain," then walked away.

"We're not done talking about this, Lieutenant."

Gage glanced back. "Understood."

He put his hand on the small of her back. As they moved out of earshot, Clare said, "Does he know about...?"

Gage was grateful she didn't say it aloud. He wasn't sure if he was ready for that so soon after McCauley's reaction. He might have no choice but to stay out of the captain's life—and the rest of his family's.

But he knew the truth that had been withheld from him for so long now.

He sighed. "We can talk about it later."

Clare nodded, a soft look on her face. "Okay."

"What did you find out from your mom? And is she okay?"

She let out a relieved breath. "Minor concussion, but she's okay. They taped it because she didn't even need stitches, but there's a lump on her head. Apparently after the cop was stabbed, her and Selena walked out of the room not knowing he was there. He hit my mom with a stun gun. She hit her head on the way down. That's when he took Selena, or so she presumes."

"A knife and a stun gun?"

She shrugged. "He knew he had to subdue Selena, get her out quietly. Maybe the knife was to threaten her."

Gage shook his head. "Did she confirm who it was?"

"Aaron, for sure."

"That's something at least."

Clare's eyes filled with tears. She looked away, her throat bobbing.

"We are going to find her."

"Where, though? And will she be dead by then?" Clare shrugged, tears sliding down her cheeks now. "I'm supposed to protect her. She's my responsibility."

"Why is that?" He figured she just cared a lot because of the connection with Selena's mother.

"Because I promised Kara I would look after her." She sniffed. "I failed. The same way I failed Kara. It's all my fault."

"You couldn't have known Selena would be his target."

"But if she's killed, it'll be on me. The way Kara's death is."

THIRTY-SEVEN

C lare swiped roughly at the tears on her face.

"You are allowed to cry, you know."

Of course he would say that. She shook her head.

Her phone rang in her pocket, but she ignored it for now. The thing had been ringing off the hook, and she needed a minute of space.

Gage dragged her against him in a hug, something they'd done many times in the past. Long ago now. Creating between them a weird mix of old and new. She'd actually admitted to someone what she knew to be true about Kara's death—that Clare's actions, her decisions, meant she was responsible.

She tucked her head against Gage's shoulder and hung on tighter than she should need to. "I haven't told Selena."

"Good. Don't."

Her phone vibrated in her pocket.

He said, "Do you need to get that?"

"No." She pulled back. "Why shouldn't I tell Selena the truth?"

"Because it's done. It's past, and she doesn't need to lose you as well as her mother."

"Shouldn't she know the truth?"

"You say it like it's a dirty secret, but if you tell her that as the team lead, it was your call. Your choice to stay or go, or whatever happened, and ultimately the people under you are your responsibility as the team leader. You think she won't already understand that on some level?"

Clare had talked a lot about the team as a whole with Selena. She'd told Kara's daughter everything about that last mission, even though maybe she shouldn't have. But she hadn't revealed the target's identity or where they were. Just how Kara had died and the circumstances.

"What if I never see her again?" Until Clare voiced it aloud, she hadn't realized how worried she was. "I can't lose someone else. Not like this."

Gage said nothing, but she read his expression anyway.

She wouldn't be responsible for this, either.

"Did your mom say anything else, other than to confirm who he is?" he finally asked.

Actionable intel? "Not much." However, she *had* said a whole lot about Selena. "Except that I shouldn't be so worked up about a girl who isn't my daughter. It isn't healthy. Like losing our baby made me so broken I latch onto anyone under my care." Clare winced. "Only, she's not wrong, is she?"

It sucked, but it was turning out that her mother really did know everything. Or most things, anyway.

Clare blew out a frustrated breath.

"You care about her. That's a good thing." Gage shrugged. "If it becomes unhealthy, you can deal with it. But Selena might need the strength of your attachment to her to keep her alive—emotionally and physically—because you're not going to stop until she's found. Right?"

Clare nodded.

He might be just saying it to make her feel better, but he was also right. How much she wanted Selena in her life might be what made the difference between success and failure.

"Clare!"

She spun to see Ember striding toward her. "Hey."

Ember launched right in. "We're scouring traffic cams around the hospital to figure out what vehicle he's driving."

"Are we sure he's not still somewhere in the hospital?"

Ember nodded. "Simon got him on camera with her over his shoulder all the way to the parking lot level of the elevator. He could've gone from there to another spot on campus, but we think it's more likely he left with her so he could recover the diamonds. Can't do that boxed in here by first responders."

Clare glanced at Gage, then said to Ember, "Find where he took her."

"We will," Ember said. "I'm praying."

Clare wasn't convinced that would help even with everything Ember had been saying the past couple of months. All about how her faith wasn't a religion, it was a relationship. If Ember wanted to talk to her heavenly Father, that was fine with Clare. Didn't mean she had to do it.

Clare would rather work the problem herself.

She knew what she could do, and she would rely on her abilities. Trust in her own strength.

"Why Vanguard?" Clare asked. "Did we figure that out?"

Her phone rang again. She didn't answer it, but checked her call history and texts. There was even a list of new emails. All about the same thing.

Ember tipped her head to the side. "Maybe. Bob has been taking a look at Aaron and his history, seeing if there's anything in his life or with someone connected to him that might've given him a reason to come after us."

Clare lifted her brows.

"Put me on the payroll later." Ember waved a hand.

"How about free lunch in the cafeteria for life?"

Ember grinned. "Deal."

"So what did he find?"

"It's not about you, or even Vanguard. There's no connection we can see. But what Bob found was connected to him." Ember glanced at Gage. "And his time as a police officer."

They moved to the side of the hall to let a couple of staff in scrubs push a bed down the hall, transporting an older man hooked up to an IV.

Clare motioned for Ember to continue.

"Aaron would've been eleven. He had an older brother." Ember stopped to collect her thoughts.

"A brother?" Gage leaned against the wall.

"He was into drugs, dealing in the neighborhood. Small-time stuff. Bob was a beat cop. One night he stops the brother and asks him to turn out his pockets. The guy is nineteen, so he's an adult. He pulls a gun instead of complying. The situation escalated, and the brother squeezed off at least one shot before Bob put him down."

Clare said, "It was ruled a good shoot?"

Ember nodded. "But who knows what Aaron thinks about the officer who killed his brother, then went to prison because it was found out that he was a dirty cop."

Gage said, "But why come after Vanguard, rather than Bob personally?"

Clare had an answer to that. "Bob was getting harassed at his apartment complex. He didn't want his daughter to know, so he told Stella it was a plumbing issue. It wasn't a good place to live, but it was all he could find when he's on probation. Anyway, I moved him into the Vanguard building."

Gage said, "You have residences?"

Clare nodded. "Top floor is all my apartment. Below me I have places for protected clients, people who need to lay low. That kind of thing. I had an empty spot, and he provides protection when he's home. Watches out for the neighbors."

When she called the code black, they'd have evacuated the man in 6B. A few of her texts had been to confirm they were out, and then confirm when they got to the new safe house.

Clare had a lot of gift card thank-yous to send when this was done.

"We think Aaron's plan was to sneak in a device," Gage said. "Or maybe pay someone to plant something."

She glanced at him. "Can we find out if Alex is awake?" The guy had extra police protection right now, but she needed to talk to him. "He's the one who knows where those diamonds are."

Gage pushed off the wall, touched her shoulder, and strode.

Ember let out a *whoo*.

Clare turned to her. "What?"

"Girl, he is fine times twelve."

Clare rolled her eyes. "I want Selena found."

"Fine, but after we get her back, we're going out for girls night again and you're gonna dish."

"Who have you become?"

"I'm a mother to a newborn. I need adult conversation, preferably juicy."

Clare sighed.

"I'm trusting God that He will keep Selena safe until we

can find her. It would be a good idea if you do the same thing, too."

"Like it's a magic trick?" Clare asked.

"You know it's not." Ember lifted her brows. "But when we admit our need for Him, that's when He can work. Until then He comes up against a wall of our stubbornness, and He's not overbearing so He won't break through it, even if I think He should sometimes. He's gentler than that. He lets us make the choice."

"Will it save her?"

"It could mean the difference between success and failure, yes," Ember said. "But it's more about your heart."

THIRTY-EIGHT

T he officer nodded. "Doc just came out. He's awake."

"You can take five," Gage said. "I need to talk to him."

"Thanks, Lieutenant." He wandered off.

They'd moved Alex to a quieter end of the hallway, away from where Aaron Crenshaw had taken Selena and stabbed another officer. A place that was easier to guard and harder to access. Though, nowhere was impenetrable.

The moment you thought like that was when you got sloppy about security.

Gage stepped into the hospital room. Things had been emotionally charged with Clare. He didn't think she would leave without him, but it was good he could do this himself. He had no stake in Selena's kidnapping other than professionally. He didn't care about her like Clare did, which meant he could ask questions without that concern lacing his tone.

"Alex, I'm Lieutenant Deluca." He left the door cracked in case Clare came looking.

The young man had been shot in the shoulder. Survived the trauma and blood loss, and surgery, and been medicated into a coma. After that, the doctors had to follow a protocol to bring him out of it. The guy was pale but looked surprisingly alert for a guy who'd nearly died recently.

"Have you been brought up to speed about what's happening?"

Alex turned to look at Gage. "I guess. He took Selena, he stabbed a cop. It's on me if she dies because I'm part of his crew." Alex's jaw flexed. "Even though I had *nothing* to do with anything after I decided to testify against him."

Gage wondered if he'd been expecting witness protection as part of a deal. "Did you believe he might do something like this?"

"He's crazy, but I didn't think he'd do this."

"Why might he have taken her?" Gage stood at the end of the bed. "Seems like something someone would do for leverage. Or are they a thing?"

Alex's nose crinkled for a second. "I know she was gonna break up with me. I mean, I could tell."

"Because they're having an affair?" That would change things, if it was true.

"They'd better not be." Alex's ire blew out quickly. "But I doubt it."

"Why's that?"

"Because he can't get to me, so he thinks she knows where the diamonds are."

"The diamonds Aaron and the crew stole from the bank," Gage said.

"Who?" Alex's brows rose.

"Aaron Crenshaw." Gage frowned. "That's his name." Alex didn't know that?

The young man frowned. "We used codes. He's Berlin. I'm Miami."

"Rio and Phoenix?" When Alex nodded, Gage asked, "What did you call the guy in the van?"

"London."

Cute. Gage nearly rolled his eyes. "So where are the diamonds?"

Alex looked away. "I have nothing to stand on if I tell you. My lawyer advised me to speak with her before I commit to anything or give you any new information. And she's getting a CT scan."

Which made him not that far from Aaron and his tactics, give or take Clare's mom and her advice. Alex might never realize it, but he was trading information in the same way Aaron would with Selena's life. But Alex probably thought he was doing the right thing.

"You've gotta give me something." Gage tried to sound desperate. "Otherwise, he calls to arrange a trade and we have nothing to give. At least get us in the ballpark, so it sounds like it makes sense."

He could say a lot of things here. Pull on tactics to get Alex to spill. But in his prayer he'd told God that he would trust Him. That he'd let the Lord work this situation out. So he had to see where Alex was at first, and then work from there.

"I hid them," Alex offered.

"At Vanguard?" No, that didn't make sense. Just because Aaron had blueprints all over his walls didn't mean that was the answer. It was no better than the chicken-and-egg debate about which came first.

Alex blinked. "How did you know?"

"I didn't." He recalled what Ember had said. "But we think Aaron—Berlin—has something against Vanguard. Do you know anything about that?"

Alex shook his head. Gage wasn't sure if he believed it,

but Alex didn't have much of a reason to lie about that right now.

"Those diamonds are what stands between Selena's life and her death. Between us being able to make a deal with Aaron for her safety and him killing her because he doesn't get what he wants." Gage studied the young man. "So where are they?"

He would leave right now and go pick them up.

Alex grimaced. "I can't tell you. But they're there, which means they're safe, right? That place is like Fort Knox. Everyone knows that. All those secret codes and Section 6-type floors."

Gage heard a tiny noise from behind the door.

"Basement, and the sub-basement with the dungeon."

He didn't want to argue, but why would Clare need a dungeon? "So you hid it there?"

"I want a written deal and assurances I'll get no jail time."

Gage frowned.

"And my lawyer signs it," Alex said. "And I want a phone so I can call my mom. She's gonna be worried *sick* about all this."

"Where would Aaron take Selena?"

Alex lifted both hands and let them fall back to the blanket. "How should I know? We only went to the house. There was nowhere else."

Gage had given it to God in prayer, so he didn't need to take it back off the altar again. *I'm trusting You have this in Your hands.*

"I'll take it from here." The door opened all the way, and Captain McCauley stepped in. "You're needed elsewhere, Lieutenant."

Gage tried to read his expression, but the guy had a blank look on his face.

In the hall, Clare motioned with a tip of her head and mouthed, *Let's go.* Maybe she'd heard what Alex said about Vanguard.

He nodded. "Thanks, Captain."

"No problem, *Lieutenant.*"

Gage ignored the tone and headed out. They could hash over their thing again later. He closed the door on McCauley and Alex, just so he could say, "Was that about me personally, or because he wants to get involved in this case?"

Clare shrugged. "Who knows?"

"Vanguard?"

"Please."

Gage didn't take her hand, but he wanted to. They took the elevator and found his car, which he drove so they could get there in record time with lights and sirens.

"I've got my people looking at the exterior cameras as much as the interior."

"You think he'll show up?"

Clare lifted her finger. "Hold on one sec." She put her phone to her ear. "Juarez." Pause. "I am. Yes, I have it in hand. No, you don't need to fly here." She sighed. "You think I don't have this?" She chuckled lightly. "Told you. But thanks, Zander. Seriously." She sighed and lowered her phone. "Sorry."

"Colleagues?"

"You wouldn't believe how many old friends are crawling out of the woodwork to offer help. Either because I'm protecting an asset of theirs, or information they're connected to, or they're just bored. Zander's baby is teething." She shot Gage a smile. "He needs a mission so he can get some rest kicking down doors and bagging suspects."

Gage snorted. "Sounds like an interesting guy."

"Do we think he'll show up to get the diamonds?"

"Or send someone like he did with the doctor. So we need to be ready for anything." Gage pulled into the parking lot of her building. "With all the personnel around, and police presence, he isn't going to be able to sneak inside. Unless you have a back door." He threw the car in park.

Clare twisted in her seat to face him. "Depends." He liked the smirk on her face. "Are you willing to sign an NDA?"

"You want a nondisclosure agreement for information about your entry and exit points?"

"Uh, *yeah*." She shook her head. "My team can work this. Don't worry. He won't get inside." She shifted in her seat. "I just want whatever happens to be fast so I can get Selena back. Every hour she's gone..."

He looked at his watch. "It's been too long."

Clare started to speak again, but his phone rang.

The screen said *Captain McCauley*. He stared for a moment, then answered, "Did Alex give you something?"

"I went to grab his lawyer." McCauley did *not* sound happy. More like this was the last thing he wanted to admit. "When I got back, he was gone."

THIRTY-NINE

The front doors slid open, and Clare pocketed her key card. She'd locked the place down, which meant no one had access but her. Alex had split from the hospital, someone else her people had to track down on surveillance cameras outside that building.

"He got into a cab." Simon edged in just before the doors closed. "Alex got into a cab outside the hospital."

"Call the company."

He nodded as he strode toward her, clutching a laptop he'd folded back on itself so she could see the keys. The screen brushed against his '70s rock T-shirt. "Gave them the number. They're contacting the driver to see if he's still in it, and where they're going. But I also called Sergeant O'Connell, and he's taking the information we give him."

"Good. Now the diamonds." Clare turned and looked around the expansive lobby, all white with little in the way of décor but a potted plant beside the couch. Not a spot where they invited people to linger, which was precisely by design.

Anyone who came here had a reason. They didn't just drop by—except for Selena, and Alex.

"Sorry?"

"If you were here and you had a small velvet pouch of diamonds, where would you put it?"

Simon walked over to the plant and kicked it over. No dirt spilled, but the plastic disk that looked like soil rattled against the floor. "In the couch, maybe?"

"Depends if he sat."

Simon shifted the laptop and tapped the screen. "Let's take a look at the footage from when they were here."

The doors opened again, and Gage walked in with Peter. There wasn't much she could do except try to find the diamonds. Until Aaron made contact, or Alex showed up—or they found him—there wasn't a move to make. Just leads to follow.

"Show me." Clare moved to the couch and glanced at Peter. "And get Sandy."

Simon settled beside her and started typing, his fingers moving about twice as fast as she could type—or anyone else she knew. "Wednesday, you were shot at in the park. Weren't you hit as well?"

Clare shrugged. "Just a graze."

Gage folded his arms. Watched. He seemed to be doing better than her facing this, but then he believed what Ember did. That God should be allowed to be in control. She had no problem with a Creator who made the world, and then left things to run. That's how she'd always thought of Him.

But the idea of talking to Him now? Or even letting go and allowing that same God to run her life?

Can I trust You? They both think I can, and I know how happy it would make them if I believed. But I have to do this for me. Not for them. I want to trust You.

Not just because she was out of options and it was worth a

shot, but because God was the only force of good in this world and she needed that in her life.

She needed to be more than what she was by herself, when no one was around.

Clare didn't like failing. Letting down people she cared about.

People she had brought under her wing. Like Selena—and the twins.

Simon glanced at her then. Now that she knew them better, it was easier to tell the difference between him and Peter, though the twins were identical. They'd had the same hair when she met them, but while Peter kept his military-short now, Simon hadn't cut his.

"Wednesday," she prompted.

He pulled up the footage and scrolled with his finger until Alex and Selena walked in. He let it play, their movements jerky. She realized he'd played it double speed. "They didn't go over to the couch. Didn't sit."

"There." Clare pointed at the screen. "He said something to Sandy."

Peter strode in, Sandy behind him.

Clare said, "What did Alex say to you, Sandy?"

Simon turned the laptop so she could see the screen.

The older woman said, "He used the restroom."

"Anything else?"

Sandy shook her head. "They weren't here more than a few minutes. I said you were out, he used the bathroom, and they left."

Clare got up and headed for the hall, using her key and holding the door when she realized Gage was right behind her.

"You think he hid the diamonds here because he thinks it's so safe?" he asked.

"Makes sense," she replied. "He didn't want to walk around with it, and he could tell the police where it is after he'd given his statement. A bargaining chip."

Gage made a face. "Why does it seem like everyone involved in this thinks they need leverage?"

She hit the men's room door with both palms and strode in, looking around. "Toilet tanks?"

"Or a trap."

She pulled out her phone and texted Simon to get Maintenance in here. She pushed open all the stall doors. Looked at the walls. There were vents high up, close to the ceiling. Difficult to reach. At the end was a closet door, just storage. She checked it, and it opened right away. "This is supposed to be locked, I think."

Just big enough for one person to turn around in, the floor was occupied by a big yellow mop bucket with two sides. Up on the shelf there was another vent. She stepped on the first shelf and grabbed the opposite side, levering herself up so she could see all the shelves.

Still holding on, she moved some things.

"There's a vent back there."

Clare saw it. "Looks like there's a screw missing."

"Was he in here long enough to do that?"

"Guess we'll find out." She shifted her foot to another shelf and lifted up high enough to pry the vent open. "Bingo."

Clare grasped the pouch and moved to get down.

Gage's hands landed on her hips, and he lowered her to the floor—and up against him.

"Thanks." The word came out far more breathy than she wanted.

His lips curled up. "Those diamonds are evidence." He lowered his head until their lips almost touched.

He saw the blush on her cheeks up close.

"He's here—oh," Simon said. "Sorry. Alex is outside, headed for the barn door."

"Thank you." She cleared her throat. "Let him inside, but tell Peter don't move in."

Clare didn't want her employees withholding important information just because they thought she was having a private moment with Gage. In a bathroom storage closet. In the middle of an intense situation.

This wasn't the time.

But when Simon turned away, she stopped long enough to clasp Gage's arm and lift up. Then planted a kiss on his cheek. She felt the reflexive squeeze of his hand on her hip.

"Hand them over," he said.

Clare dropped the pouch into his hand.

Gage checked the contents and pocketed it. "I need an evidence bag."

When she reached the hall, Simon lifted his hand to his ear. "Okay." He glanced at her and she continued, "Peter has him in the barn."

"He had Selena's card," Gage said.

"Okay." Clare strode ahead of him. She shoved open the doors to the barn, which was basically a garage and the whole ground floor behind the lobby. Rows of cars of all kinds, new and old. Vans, little two-seater vintage sports cars. Her motorcycle. Peter's Ducati. Bob's beat-up pickup truck. An entire row of armored SUVs.

Alex crept toward them along the wall, about to run.

"Why waste my time making me chase you?" Clare asked. She spotted Peter behind Alex. "Besides, you're boxed in."

He blinked.

She strode right up to him, knowing she had backup. "Start talking."

"He'll kill her." Alex gasped, tears filling his eyes. "I have to get the diamonds before..."

Gage stepped up beside her. "Before what?"

If Clare had to guess, it probably had to do with whatever the schematics had been for. "You don't get the diamonds until you tell us everything." As if she would give them to him.

"I have to get out by ten after. That's the cutoff." He looked at his watch. "I have to be clear of the building by then." He shifted, agitated and in a hurry.

Gage said, "What will happen at ten after?"

"The whole building is gonna explode."

FORTY

"Roll the bomb squad. Now." Gage gripped the phone and paced to the front doors. They had to get everyone out. He spun back, half listening to the department dispatcher. "Clear the building!" He moved the phone away from his ear. "Everyone out!"

Her people started to move.

Gage palmed his cuffs with his other hand, sliding them off his belt.

Alex saw.

"Gotta go." He hung up the phone. "You're under arrest." He dragged the young man to the door. "Let's go!"

No way was Gage going to let anyone get caught in here when there were barely minutes to spare until a possible explosion took out the entire building.

"You are not sending the bomb squad over." Clare's voice filtered over from behind him.

"Everyone needs to move back! There could be a bomb! No one goes inside!" Gage used his "lieutenant on crowd control" voice. "Everyone back!"

People started to murmur.

"It's okay, everyone!"

He spun to see Clare had raised her hands. "Okay? We need to get these people back." He put cuffs on Alex as he spoke.

She strode over. "We don't need the bomb squad." She spun back. "Simon?"

"Yes, ma'am." The IT department twin tapped the screen of his laptop. He already knew what to do?

"Wanna loop me in?" Gage said.

Clare set her hand on her hip. "Like you did before you called the bomb squad? We have no idea where the device is. You think I'm gonna let a bunch of cops traipse through my building?"

"I think they use robots, actually."

Alex grunted. Not quite a laugh but enough to draw Clare's attention. She shot a glare at him, then, "Jesus, help us."

"Amen." Gage softened. "We need everyone away from the building. No one goes inside."

"And we need to find a bomb, before it explodes." She turned away and strode to Simon, looking over his shoulder. He heard *firecracker* and *protocol* but nothing else.

Gage strode with Alex to his car, where he had the guy sit on the hood of his vehicle.

People moved away from the building. A few got in their cars and left.

The Vanguard building had no signage outside. Only one directory listing on the entrance to the complex, and nothing where he'd have thought huge lettering should be attached to the side of the building.

Maybe they didn't really want to be found.

Clare talked to a couple of people, touching elbows and giving out warm smiles. Apparently they weren't so concerned about the possible incendiary device. Then she turned and walked toward him, and he saw the truth on her face. She was terrified—but she'd put on a polite smile as the leader of the company.

Gage softened a little.

Clare strode all the way over until she was face-to-face with Alex. "How did you contact him?"

Gage had been wondering the same thing.

Alex started to bluster.

"You called him." Gage glared. "He couldn't have called you because you had no cell phone. So what number did you dial?"

Alex stayed completely still.

Clare said, "If you want Selena back—"

Alex cut her off. "It's a burner. He made us memorize the number. He was weird about random stuff like that."

"Where are you supposed to bring the diamonds?" Clare folded her arms.

Alex flinched. "You found them."

Neither he nor Clare mentioned they were currently tucked in Gage's pocket.

"Where is Selena?" Gage asked, even though he didn't know for sure Alex had that information. The guy needed to know they were going to make saving his girlfriend a priority. Recovery of the diamonds was almost incidental. Plus, it seemed like Vanguard had the explosive device issue in hand.

Right then, a guy emerged from the back of a van, dressed in a bomb suit. He walked over to Simon and Peter, and they talked while someone else used a remote control to get a robot out of the van, down a ramp onto the ground.

"I have to call him," Alex said, "and we're gonna make the trade."

Gage winced. "You realize last time your friend made that

arrangement, he dropped the girl off early so she could die before anyone found her?" Though, thankfully they'd saved the doctor's wife. "We need to set the location so we can control every inch of this operation."

"So you're gonna call him back," Clare told Alex.

"And you're gonna tell him *exactly* what we tell you to say," Gage added. "No deviations."

"Okay." Alex hung his head. "I just want her safe. Whether she wants me anymore or not."

Clare said, "There's an abandoned factory on Arlington Road. You'll meet him there and nowhere else, but he can set the time. Let him decide that so he thinks he has some control."

Gage nodded. "He might balk at your location. But feed him a line about having no car. You've got to walk there, and that's close."

"He'll know something is up."

"Not if you don't let him," Gage said. "If he wants the diamonds, he'll come."

"He wants the diamonds." Clare nodded.

Simon called to someone.

The guy jogged back from ushering people away from the building and pointing across the parking lot. More people had left. Someone had looped in emergency services because a fire truck pulled into the parking lot and pulled up on the far side, as away from the building as they could get. Two police cars followed it.

They worked out the script for Alex and had him make the call. Aaron Crenshaw never answered the phone, so Alex laid it all out in a voicemail. When he'd hung up, Alex said, "I hope that works."

Gage said, "I pray it does."

Simon spun to them. "Clare!" When she twisted around to look at him, he yelled, "Package delivery yesterday!"

Gage passed off Alex to the officers, who stuck him in their back seat and confirmed they wouldn't let him out of their sight. Then he ran to Simon and Peter.

One twin started. "But if we do that—"

"I know, but—" The other caught the thought and continued it.

The first one finished. "Maybe. If it works."

Gage turned to Clare. "What just happened?"

"Let them work it," she said—more to the bomb squad guy than him.

"Someone needs to go in and get it." Gage figured they could lead the robot at least. "No one will see all your secrets."

Simon looked at Clare. "We can take it downstairs and incinerate it."

Gage frowned.

Clare looked at him. "It's for burning sensitive documents. Nothing else."

He let his brows rise. Peter smirked.

The bomb squad guy said, "Tell me where it is."

Simon looked at Clare. She nodded. They gave the suited-up sergeant an earpiece, and Simon directed him to a room behind the lobby, up an elevator hidden behind the wall just for deliveries. "He found it."

Gage moved closer to Simon and looked over his shoulder at the surveillance feed on his screen. "And you have a place to destroy it?"

"In the sub-basement," Clare said. "Next door to the dungeon."

No one laughed.

"He'll be done in a moment." Peter rocked back and forth on his tactical boots while Simon led the bomb squad tech through a basement hall, carrying the package to an inciner-ator where he disposed of it.

No one spoke until the bomb tech called, "All clear."

"Oka—" Clare began, just as an explosion blew out windows on the third floor.

Everyone ducked. Peter pulled Simon down with him.

Another blast blew out windows on the fifth floor. On the feed, he saw the bomb tech guy head for a door marked STAIRS.

Then another bomb exploded at the top on the far side—just under the top floor of the building where she said she'd lived.

Clare sucked in a breath. No one spoke the obvious aloud. *There was more than one bomb.* She said, "Multiple packages."

"I was only looking for one." Simon turned to Clare. "I didn't think there would be more."

She touched his shoulder. "No one is hurt. Bob isn't even here, and everyone is out of the building."

The bomb tech guy hoofed it up the stairs faster than Gage thought he should be able to go wearing all that protec-tive gear.

"Lieutenant Deluca!"

Gage spotted the officer, jogging over. "What is it, Omara?"

"Your guy got a text." He handed Gage the phone.

Gage read it and looked at Clare. "He wants the woman from the bank to deliver the diamonds."

Clare's eyes flared. "Good." She clapped her hands together. "We're gonna get this guy."

FORTY-ONE

A ll that bravado got Clare to the meeting spot without her hands shaking too badly. Now she was here—down the street, anyway—and ready to go get Selena? She felt like a brand-new recruit on her first day.

"Weapon?"

Clare wanted to say yes to Gage and accept the .22 she had a slim holster for. Instead, she shook her head. Not worth the risk. This was the man who'd bombed her building, causing destruction on multiple floors.

"Clare."

She pressed down the tape on her vest and turned only her head. "What?"

Gage stood at the back of his car. He'd geared up as well, but wasn't going in. She had to go alone—per Aaron's instructions. Later she wanted to investigate more of the things he had in the back of his car. Right now she wanted to get in and save Selena.

If she could.

"I need to go." She stepped back. "We good?"

The gold in his eyes glinted. "We pray first."

She wanted to tell him no, but since he and Ember both stood firm in their beliefs and she had recently started to pray, she took his hand and shifted close. There were a few minutes until she had to be in there, but she didn't want to wait that long.

"Amen." Gage kissed her forehead.

"I have to go."

His lips lingered against the skin of her forehead. "I know." He sighed. "Go get Selena. SWAT will be here in minutes to back us up."

Clare said, "Stay out of sight. He said I have to come alone."

Since she didn't want to get into a protracted argument about her abilities, Clare pushed away and strode down the sidewalk to the building she owned. Actually, Clare owned most of the block. They used this place for urban response training, and to have dart gun wars when they needed to blow off steam.

Her building hadn't been destroyed. She could make repairs to what had been damaged by those small explosions. On multiple floors. Clare winced. *Your house is probably fine.* One day she wouldn't live on the highest level of her office building, but right now she liked the convenience.

The center building here, the one that had been a church once, had a particle board door. The padlock had been busted off by local kids. Clare had never bothered repairing it since there wasn't anything inside to steal. Once in a while she had someone check the place wasn't being used as a flop house.

Leaves littered the floor inside the tiny vestibule. Pews had been pushed over, the padding sliced and torn. A hymnal lay discarded on the floor. One of the stained-glass windows had been smashed out, and they'd covered it with wood. Little light filtered through from the streetlamps outside.

She knew where power had been connected, and which light switches worked.

Clare flipped on a flashlight and shined it around. "Hello?"

A rustle in the far corner caught her attention. Clare pretended she didn't know there was anything there. "Hello?"

"Clare?" The voice sounded faraway, tinny like a speaker.

"Selena!" Clare moved faster down the center aisle of the sanctuary.

"Clare!" Definitely coming through a phone speaker.

She found the mobile device on the front pew. A video call displaying Selena, bound with a gag below her chin as though she'd shifted it off her face.

Clare lifted the phone but kept her attention on the sanctuary around her. Selena wasn't here—she was somewhere else. The background of the video call wasn't here or any of the buildings around her, or the basements and tunnels below.

"Are you okay?"

Selena started to cry. She had a bruise on her cheekbone, and blood at the corner of her mouth. "You need to come get me."

"I will, honey. I promise."

Someone started to laugh, low and mean. The phone shifted. "You expected things to go smoothly, I guess?"

"Hardly." Aaron had surprised them multiple times so far. Clare walked back to the front of the building.

"You tell anyone, I kill her." Aaron held a knife to Selena's throat. Stained with blood. The knife he'd used on that cop?

"So far you haven't killed anyone. That I know of. You probably want to keep it that way unless you want the cops to hunt you down." She figured they would hunt him down anyway, but it would be good if he got complacent and messed up. It would make their job a whole lot easier.

"You want her back."

"And you want the diamonds," she countered. "So why the runaround? Tell me where you are."

"Mile marker seven. Ditch the cop."

Clare walked to a credenza in the vestibule to grab a pencil. "And then?"

"Walk a mile up the trail, there's a cabin. The girl will be inside."

"Anything else?"

Selena stared to speak. She got out barely a cry before Aaron ended the call. Clare's stomach clenched. She looked out a gap in the front door and spotted the rest of Gage's SWAT team. If he rolled up to the cabin with her, Aaron could get spooked and kill Selena.

Clare only needed a few minutes' head start.

SWAT moved to surround the building.

She headed for the back exit and raced across the grass behind the old church. In the trees, she sent Gage a text that she was all right. Selena wasn't here.

She ran through the trees to the garage behind the house two doors down. An old Pontiac sat in the garage. It barely ran, but she prayed then and hotwired it.

The ignition caught, and the car rumbled to life.

Her phone started to ring. *Gage calling.*

Instead of answering, she texted him the information Aaron had given her. She'd have a couple of minutes at best, Gage would be right behind her, and the SWAT team would be mad. But they'd back her up.

Clare bit her lip. She wanted to pray on the way to the mile marker, but the words didn't want to come. Selena needed to be saved, and Clare was the one who had to do it.

For Kara.

If God wanted to help her with it, then that was His

prerogative. It wouldn't work unless God wanted a relationship with her as much as she might want one with Him. Relationships had to have balance. Ember had told her God was overwhelming with His love, and Clare had to admit she wanted to know what that felt like.

Give me peace, God.

Her phone rang again. Clare left it in the car and hoofed it up the trail, clutching the phone that had been in the church.

The cabin looked like a half-a-million-dollar structure that had been finished only a month ago. The weather had barely touched the exterior, and the surrounding grass still had lines between each strip of sod.

Definitely new.

Clare walked up the porch steps where someone had planted bulbs in pots that flanked the front door. Tiny green buds poked through the potting soil. Before she could knock on the front door, it opened.

Aaron Crenshaw held a gun, pointed at her. "Leave all your weapons outside."

Clare spread her hands. "You said not to bring one, so I didn't."

"Prove it."

She shifted her jacket off her shoulders and dropped it to the porch. The crisp temperature made her shiver. She then raised the hem of her shirt and turned all the way around.

"Pants."

She lifted her foot and raised the hem, showing him there was nothing holstered at her ankle. Then she did the same with the other. She lowered her foot and straightened. Hands spread. "Where is Selena?"

"Inside." He motioned with the gun. "You'd better have the diamonds."

Clare had the pouch in her pants pocket. "Selena first."

"Get inside."

She moved her fingers out of sight, stepped into the cabin, and looked around. She turned back to him.

The gun came down on her forehead.

Clare's tiny can of mace clattered to the entryway tile, and everything went black.

FORTY-TWO

"E asy." Liam got in his face.

Gage pocketed the phone—probably better than throwing it, which was what he wanted to do. He slammed the door shut. Liam had parked behind Clare's vehicle.

"At least she told us where to go." Blake shrugged the strap of his rifle over his shoulders so it lay across his body and left his hands free. "So let's go."

Gage grunted. "Fine."

Liam shot him a look, and Gage took off running. They hit the trail in formation and sprinted as a group. Surrounded by his guys, Gage felt the presence of God in the fellowship he had with his brothers. They didn't believe the way he did, but he'd been talking to them about what he'd found in God.

What Clare might also have found.

He'd heard her prayer and wanted to believe she had started to lean on Him. God had proven He was near to the brokenhearted. Never before in his life had Gage felt the peace that permeated his life now.

He'd never been satisfied or felt loved. Or seen himself as worthy.

But, God.

There wasn't much else to say aside from that.

The rest of the verse said that He saved those who were crushed in spirit. Which was exactly how he'd been when things ended with Clare. His life wouldn't be free of things that could crush him or leave him brokenhearted again. But having God near made all the difference.

"Cabin," Blake called out, then he and Jasper split.

Blake ran left. Jasper went right. Liam stuck with Gage. It wasn't right that Dakota wasn't here, but Gage prayed his friend could heal. That he would find the truth. There was a residency place in Last Chance County that treated veterans for PTSD, where Dakota could find a program to help him.

Another thing to pray for.

Gage headed for the front door. "Anything?"

Blake said, "Clear."

There was no response from Jasper.

"Jas?"

"Suspect in the trees, fleeing northeast. I'm in pursuit." His voice was breathy, like he was running.

Liam took off after him. "On my way."

"Blake, go with. I'll clear the cabin and catch up." Gage wanted to know if Clare was inside.

He hit the front steps at a run, a prayer on his lips, then shoved the door open, gun first. Cleared it before he looked at the floor in front of him.

Clare lay in a heap on the entryway tile, eyes closed. He kept part of his attention on the room around him and crouched. Shook her shoulder.

"Clare, wake up." He put one knee down.

She moaned and rolled onto her back. Her eyes fluttered open.

"It's just me." He didn't want her to react in a panic and get scared. She had enough training she could hurt him in a way that made him respect her a whole lot.

She gasped, and her hands moved to her pockets.

"He took the diamonds?" Gage wanted to be mad at her, but if it'd been her that was captured, he'd have done the same thing.

Clare sat up. "You tell me."

Gage wanted to chuckle, but it wasn't exactly the time. "Fine. I dumped them out into a different bag and gave you dirt from outside Vanguard to trade."

"We need to find Selena. Later we can talk about how you lied and didn't trust me."

He shifted back on his heels and stood, they clasped hands, and he hauled her to her feet. "Really? Cause that's gonna be an interesting conversation." Considering she'd done the same thing.

They broke off from each other and circled the cabin.

"Nice place."

She didn't reply to his comment.

Gage checked the bedroom, as there was only one. Huge king-size bed and fancy shiny material comforter. Ornate headboard that would hurt like the dickens if you whacked your head on it getting into bed too fast. Or sitting up too fast. He had a tiny scar on his forehead from doing that when he was a kid. It'd bled like crazy.

"Pantry is clear. Where else is—"

Gage pushed open the door to the bathroom. "Got her."

Selena lay in the tub, tied up. Eyes closed. Too many bumps and scars on her. He crouched and pressed two fingers to her neck. Her eyes flew open.

Gage pulled the tape from her mouth. Clare disappeared and came back with scissors, which she used to cut Selena free of the zip ties around her wrists and ankles. Her clothes were rumpled but didn't look like they'd been removed. Aaron hadn't hurt Katrina like that—as far as she'd told Clare—and he prayed the same was true of Selena.

"I couldn't save myself." Tears filled Selena's eyes. One slipped down her cheek.

Clare crouched beside him and gripped the edge of the bath. "That's why you have us, honey."

Gage nodded. She couldn't possibly think they expected her to have rescued herself and got away. Gage and Clare were both trained, and they couldn't get free of everything. "We all need help sometimes."

"Even if needing help sucks all the time." Clare chuckled, but it sounded hollow. She reached over and hauled Selena to her feet. She glanced at Gage. "Maybe you could go get the car."

Gage agreed it would be faster than calling an ambulance to come all the way out here, and Selena needed to get checked out at the hospital. "The guys are catching up with Aaron. They'll find him." He needed to get on the radio and see how that was going.

From what he could hear, they'd been closing in. Now they were out of range of the signal that connected their earpieces together.

Gage wanted to catch up and help, almost as much as he knew he needed to stay here. "Okay. You guys sit in the living room and I'll go get the car." To Selena he said, "Can you walk?"

She frowned. The young woman seemed to be slower to consider his question, so he wondered if she'd had a concussion.

"Come on." He needed her to lift her leg and step out of the bath. Whether she could do that or not would tell him a lot of what he needed to know.

"He..." She shook her head, her eyes rolling back.

Gage reached for Selena, shifted the rifle to his back, then lifted her in his arms. "Okay. I got you."

"Aaron..." Her voice trailed off, and she choked on a sob.

"I know. He's not going to hurt you anymore." Gage laid her on the couch and saw she looked a lot better than he'd thought at first. He did a quick assessment. Heart rate. Breathing. Pupils. He glanced at Clare. "What happened?"

"There was a phone in the church," Clare said. "He told me no cops, but I wasn't going to do that because I'm not someone who goes in with no backup."

Gage nodded. "So you texted me."

"I figured a couple minutes' head start was enough to fool him into thinking I was alone." She pressed her lips together.

Thankfully she didn't mention how he'd lied to her about the diamonds. They were probably even since she'd done the same, ditching him and going off alone.

Gage keyed his radio. "Status report, Sergeant."

Clare waited. Then she said, "Anything?"

"I have no idea if they've caught him yet or not."

"Do you need to go?"

"I need info, but they can handle one guy." Before, he'd have gone after them and made sure they were okay. Now he wasn't sure if it said more about his need to be near to Clare and make sure she was all right than any kind of letting go of control with his men.

Something he could unpack later.

Though, considering he'd opted to give all the worry to God and let Him handle it, maybe this was that answer to prayer.

He looked at Clare. "I'm trusting that I'm where I need to be."

Her expression softened in a way he liked a whole lot. "Thank you."

"Let's get Selena out of here." He stood.

"Maybe we will come with you and hang out outside. I don't like being in here when Aaron was so quick to leave."

"You think he set a bomb?"

"If he did, I don't want to risk it." She tugged on Selena's arms. "Come on, honey."

He helped her stand and took her weight while Clare held the door open.

Two steps across the porch, and the cabin exploded.

The force shoved them off the porch. Selena slipped from his arms, and they hit the ground. Clare landed on the back of his legs and screamed. Everything in him reacted to her, wanting to reach for her. Talk to her. Hold onto her.

He reached for her, and the world swallowed up into black.

FORTY-THREE

Clare blinked awake, lying in a hospital bed. IV in her arm. Covers up to her chin. Her mother in the chair beside her. "Mom."

Letitia's eyes blinked open, and she sat forward in the chair. "Hey, honey."

That word brought everything flooding back. She remembered Selena in the bathtub, and the cabin exploding. She shifted in the bed, and pain shot down her leg.

"Easy." Letitia stood and laid her hand on Clare's arm. "You broke your ankle. You'll need to keep still for a while."

Clare said, "Selena. Gage."

Letitia nodded. "They're both here." Her eyes were slightly glassy. She'd been hit in the head just a day or so ago. Now she was up. "Gage was knocked out. Selena woke up first, and she's being treated. There are cops here taking her statement."

"What about Aaron? Did they catch him?"

Letitia shuddered. "I hope so, but I hadn't heard yet."

The door opened, and Ember stuck her head in. "Oh, I'll come back. But I'm glad you're awake."

"Come in." Letitia waved a hand, and her gold bracelet slid down from her wrist. "Please."

Ember closed the door. She came over. "You okay?"

Clare was more inclined to tell Ember the truth than her own mother, but the sad fact was that Ember had earned that place in Clare's heart. Her mother had always kept her at arms' length, as though the point was to prove to people you were better than them.

Like Gage.

Her mother hadn't wanted Clare to date him in the first place. Which was a lot of the reason Clare had responded to him. A small act of rebellion that lasted a minute until she realized that the most good-looking guy in sophomore year was also a great guy.

The way joining the army had been a rebellion. The furthest thing from what her mother wanted her to do—and that was exactly what she did.

Her thoughts inevitably drifted back to Gage. Who made a point to be kind these days? She'd seen him showing kindness to a kid who was bullied and fallen hard. Part of her had loved him every day since. Even when she thought he walked out on her.

"I'd like to say I can't believe you offered Gage money to leave me." Clare shook her head at her mother. "But I can absolutely believe it."

Ember gasped. "You didn't." She coughed. "I mean, sorry."

"No." Letitia actually shook her head. "You shouldn't be. The truth is, it's me that should be sorry." She shrugged. "Only, partly I'm not. You didn't need to be in a relationship that young. It was a sure thing, and I knew it."

Maybe her mother would never completely come around. She would always be true to who she was, but it did make

Clare feel better that she at least admitted she *should* be sorry. Even if she wasn't. "Thank you for saying that."

Things weren't always perfect. Actually, Clare wondered if maybe they were almost never perfect. Right now she was content for just this moment with her mother.

Ember leaned against the bed.

"How is my building?" Clare asked.

Ember actually winced. "No structural damage that we can tell, but an inspector needs to confirm that. The damage looked mostly cosmetic."

"Where did Aaron get bombs?" She hadn't been able to figure that part out.

"We found a guy in town. Like the laundromat people he killed, the guy and his secretary. There was another homicide the police were investigating. A man who contracts that kind of thing. There was a payment between him and Aaron. We confirmed all the bombs are accounted for. They all went off."

"The cabin?"

Ember nodded. "That one was on a timer. I think he wanted Selena, you and whoever else showed up dead in there. Maybe he thought he'd get away."

"Did the cops catch him?"

"I asked Captain McCauley. He said Sergeant O'Connell was bringing the suspect in."

She'd figured they would shoot him. But if they'd arrested him, then Selena—and everyone else affected—would see justice. "Good."

"The crew killed one of their group, but the other four are all in custody."

Clare pushed out a breath. "That's really good."

"Don't worry," Letitia said, "I won't offer to represent all of them."

Clare nearly snorted. "Thanks. I appreciate that."

"I'm going to go check on Selena. She was talking about having to go to the police station to break up with Alex." Letitia leaned down and kissed Clare's cheek. "I'm glad you're going to be all right."

"And if I start dating Gage?" Clare winced, not planning to say that aloud necessarily. "Will you still be glad, or will you try and pay him off again?"

"You know he didn't take it, right?"

Clare nodded. Ember let out a tiny snort.

Letitia continued, "You're an adult, Clare. Make your own choices. I love you, so I'll support whatever you decide. I just want you to be happy."

"Thanks, Mom." Clare smiled. "I love you, too."

Letitia waved a hand and let herself out.

"Huh." Ember grinned and pulled up a chair. "You good? I can go see if Gage is awake if you want to talk to him."

"We have time." She wasn't in a hurry, and moving wouldn't feel too good right now. "You know how you said that it's not religion, it's a relationship?"

Ember stilled. "Yes."

"Do you think maybe you could explain some more of that? Because I trusted God in the heat of the moment, and I don't know what would have happened if I hadn't. But I believe He did come through. I mean, we're all alive right? We could be dead. Selena could've been dead." Clare didn't want to think about that. Her eyes filled with traitorous tears she didn't like.

"That happened to me a lot when I became a Christian."

Clare frowned. "What?"

"Crying."

"Ugh." Ember had mentioned that before.

Ember chuckled. "You've had a hard heart for years. Trying to protect yourself from being hurt again. Now you're softening and God comes in, flooding everything with care and kindness. Suddenly we have tons of empathy, and we hurt for other people."

"That sounds like it's not a good thing."

"It is."

"Hmm." Clare didn't like the idea of getting all sappy just because God thought she needed to care too much. She had her circle and she would give everything for those people. It wasn't about needing to sacrifice to make up for what they'd lost.

Or what she'd cost them.

Now it was more about the pure love she had for people like Selena, and Gage. Her family and friends, and the coworkers she loved like they were friends and family. The same sentiment, now for a whole different reason.

She didn't need to atone.

God had already done that for her.

And while she could do everything to make sure Selena had a support network, it wasn't about obligation. It was because she loved that young woman like family.

"You won't regret making the choice to follow God," Ember said. "Like you won't regret choosing to take a chance on Gage."

"We haven't even talked about dating." And yet, her heart had already decided, hadn't it? She wasn't going to bother trying to be logical when her emotions were involved, as much as she wanted to use caution and wait for God to lay the path out ahead of her.

She wanted to talk to Gage. Tell him how she felt about him—still.

"But you're both thinking about it." Ember lifted her brows. "And more."

"Just because you're hurrying to get married doesn't mean everyone is."

"Like you'd say no." Ember chuckled and stood. "I'll go check in with Bob and Pete. Start planning the renovations."

"I want everything back where it was." Clare looked around. "And I need my phone. It was in my car."

"I'll check on that. Track it down." Ember reached the door. "Arlington Street?"

Clare nodded, because that was where she'd left her vehicle. "And...Ember?"

"Yeah?"

"Can you bring me a Bible?" If she was going to lie here, she would at least do something useful.

Ember grinned. "On it."

The door closed.

In the quiet, Clare shut her eyes and let go of the hold she'd had on her broken heart. God could take those pieces and make something whole. The way she wanted to be when she told Gage that she loved who he was now even more than she'd loved the boy he'd been back then.

God, You can write the next chapter of this story. I trust You.

FORTY-FOUR

G age flipped the shoulder of his shirt on. He had to stop and take a breath, let it out slowly. His ribs were cracked, not broken, thankfully. Didn't mean it didn't *hurt.* The ER bustled around him, but he ignored it, hidden behind the curtain the nurse had pulled before she had him take off his shirt so she could see.

He sighed, then started buttoning the shirt.

Liam had shown up at the cabin after it exploded, Aaron with him in cuffs. Those darn pipe bombs in cardboard boxes Aaron had used to blow up parts of Vanguard. He'd stashed one at the house so he could get away and destroy all the evidence in the process.

Liam had gone to the PD to book Aaron Crenshaw. Blake and Jasper had gone with him because Gage insisted on it—and had to pull rank to get them to go when they didn't after he insisted.

They'd told him after he woke up, before the orders, that it looked like Clare had broken her leg. Selena had been unconscious and beat-up. He figured it was likely the mental healing would take longer than the physical.

All was right in the world. So why did he feel like they'd barely started? Not with the case. The bank robbers were caught, or dead.

The curtain moved, and he spotted Dakota. Nervous.

Gage said, "Get in here. I need help." He let his hands fall to his lap.

Dakota let the curtain fall behind him and came over. "Help with what?"

Everything. "Where are my shoes?"

Dakota huffed a laugh. "You're sure you shouldn't be admitted?" The guy looked like he wanted to test Gage's forehead for a fever. "You don't look so good."

"I'm fine. I just need shoes."

"So you can go talk to Clare?" Dakota eyed him. "Might want to wait for that."

"I don't want to."

Dakota chuckled. He pulled open a cupboard by the bed and found a big clear plastic bag with Gage's things in it. He straightened but didn't hand it over. For a long moment Dakota stared at him. "I need help."

Gage's chest tightened in a way that had nothing to do with the cracked ribs.

"Thank you for suspending me." Dakota looked at the bag in his hands. "I called my brother, Will. We talked for a while."

"Did you decide anything?"

"He said there's this place. A therapy center for veterans, and they'll take a washed-up cop. He's gonna try and get me into their residency program as soon as possible. It's in Last Chance County."

Gage nodded. "The Ridgeman Center. That's a great idea, Dakota."

Dakota nodded as well, like he didn't know what else to do.

Gage put out his hand. Dakota shook it, but Gage used the hold on his friend to lever himself up to standing. He only let out a tiny groan when it hurt. Gage pulled Dakota into a hug. "Bro."

Dakota hung on. They slapped each other's backs.

"You need anything, give me a call," Gage said. "And I mean anything, *ever*."

Dakota nodded. There was more slapping, and then Dakota was gone.

Gage still didn't know how he was going to bend over and slip his feet into his boots. He tied the laces loosely and dropped the first boot on the floor. Wiggled his foot into it.

"Aren't you a sorry sight."

Gage twisted around so hard he nearly passed out.

"Whoa." Dennis McCauley strode in far enough to put a hand on Gage's shoulder.

He breathed and tried not to pass out.

"There's someone here who wants to see you're okay. I'll give you a second, though."

Gage looked up, then just stared when McCauley didn't move. He had no idea what to say. "I'm not going to turn your life inside out."

"You think I wasn't blindsided?" McCauley took half a step back and folded his arms. "But I figure from the look on your face that you were as well."

Gage said nothing.

"The old man is the only one who doesn't seem to be surprised." McCauley shook his head. "Though, I guess he was there." He winced. "You know what I mean."

Gage realized the captain was as flustered as he was. "Look, McCauley—"

"Yeah, we're gonna have to figure all that out, *Gage*."

"That's just weird. Deluca is fine. Or *lieutenant*."

"Yeah, 'cause I can call you *lieutenant* at Thanksgiving dinner." McCauley chuckled. "We just need to embrace the awkward. Jeanie—that's my sister, the one you met—can get over it. She'll love the drama of the whole thing once she realizes you're all right. And my wife will have someone else to mother. She'll send you smoothie recipes and ask about your health regimen." He patted his stomach. "If you're eating enough greens."

Gage couldn't help but smile.

"And the kids will have someone else who can help keep them in line." McCauley must've read Gage's face because he said, "Two girls. Fourteen and twelve. So get ready for that firestorm." He must've thought that was hilarious.

Gage wasn't sure he wanted to know.

"Anyway, Pops wants to see you, and I left him in a chair while I cleared the air, so..."

"Thanks." Gage nodded.

McCauley nodded back. "You should sit with us at church on Sunday. Lunch after at my house. We'll go from there." The tone sounded an awful lot like Captain McCauley orders. Honestly, that made Gage feel better.

"Okay...Dennis."

McCauley disappeared, then reappeared as Alistair shuffled in, staying by the curtain while his father came over.

"Son."

Gage didn't know what to do.

Alistair set his hand on Gage's shoulder. "You good, Son?"

Gage nodded. The lump in his throat stuck there.

Alistair tugged him forward, and when their heads touched, he squeezed the back of Gage's neck.

All Gage could do was not breathe for a second while he got his first hug from his father.

Alistair stayed there probably longer than was necessary.

Gage grabbed a handful of his old man's shirt and held on for dear life, gasping when he should've been cool. And yet, he didn't care at all that he was on the verge of breaking down.

Thank You, Lord.

Gage had been given something he'd never had. So he didn't know what losing it felt like, just what it'd felt like to lose his mom.

This was a gift—pure and simple. The goodness of God regardless of the status of his birth and how he came to be. What his mom had told him over and over, that he wasn't good enough to be accepted by people.

Gage had strived for so long. Proving himself. Building a career. Gaining rank and becoming team leader.

All the things that meant something in his life hadn't come about because of any work he'd done. They were all gifts. Blessings. Things God had given him that proved His goodness, and proved He had a plan all along for Gage's life. That He had always been there, and He'd never—not once— failed to look out for Gage.

Thank You.

All along God had been working in his life.

Help me with this now. Please, Lord.

Gage leaned back, still hanging on to his dad. "How do you convince a woman to take a chance on you?"

Alistair McCauley touched Gage's face, his thumb moving over Gage's cheek. "She worth it?"

"She always has been. But she didn't know it."

Alistair nodded. "Sounds like there's work to do."

FORTY-FIVE

Three weeks later

Clare shook her head. "That's crazy, right?"

Gage gripped the steering wheel. "Your mom does seem like maybe she's trying to change."

He seemed kind of nervous, which he hadn't been since she got out of the hospital. In the last couple of weeks, she'd had multiple meetings with the police department, signing paperwork for Vanguard to officially become a contractor.

Hobbling in and out on crutches because she had a broken ankle had been irritating but seemed to help the PD's view of her. She'd been injured in the line of duty according to them.

She and Gage had hung out there until she was released. At that point her people had already finished repairs on her apartment—which they'd started with—and Bob's. From there they headed downstairs, making fixes as they went. Cleaning up and replacing drywall.

Selena had moved in as soon as she was released as well. Clare had fixed up a guest room for her, and the young woman had helped her get ready for more than one date with

Gage. Clare just needed to figure out how to tell Selena what she'd found out about the girl's missing father.

Picking out an outfit for a fancy dinner had been worse than being pinned down behind enemy lines—or talking about family. She'd told Selena a story of one time Clare and Kara had been at a bar in Hawaii and Selena had laughed herself silly over her mother's antics.

And then she'd laughed even more at the idea Clare started the whole thing.

Her mother's actions were the most confusing part of the last few weeks. Instead of going back to Seattle, her mother had signed contracts on a house in the hills outside Benson and declared she was moving back to town.

The whole thing was bizarre—more than Gage's nervousness right now.

She frowned at him. "What's up?"

"Talked to my dad today."

"Okay."

Gage had been working long shifts this last week, taking care of a gang case that turned into hostages and the whole thing had been a mess. He waded in and settled tense situations like it was nothing. But ask the man to watch rice while it cooked? You'd think she asked him to hijack a container ship.

He pulled off the road into a wide driveway.

"You know the person who lives here?" She'd helped him clean out his mom's house, and Gage had put it up for sale. Maybe he used the money to buy this place. He had a condo, but maybe he wanted space.

"This is the McCauley family home."

"Oh. Is this where we're having dinner?"

Clare had met Alistair once, when they visited his home at the retirement center. He seemed like a nice guy who genuinely cared about his son, and who wanted to make up for the wrong he'd done. Gage's mother was the one who'd shut Alistair out of his life, not allowing him to give Gage anything. He'd been denied access to his son.

"Dad talked to Dennis and Jeanie. He's giving me the house. He says I can do whatever I want with it, sell it or live here." Gage turned off the car but didn't get out. "Start a family here."

Clare felt her brows rise.

"Let's go inside." He grabbed some keys and got out.

She followed him to the front door, and he let her in. "Your half-brother and sister don't want the house?"

"Apparently they agreed with him. Alistair paid for their college, but he was denied helping me out. Or having a relationship with me. He wants to do this, and they think it's a great idea, apparently."

Clare looked around the entryway. "It's a nice house." *In a nice neighborhood.* Not terribly snooty like the one she'd grown up in, but not rundown.

"Fancy but not so fancy it's pretentious." Gage made a face.

"Like my house when I was growing up?" She waited a beat. "Because it *was* ridiculous. Mom is now buying a far-too-big, far-too-fancy place in the mountains so she can call it 'the cottage.' Like it's quaint."

He chuckled. "Right."

Gage set his hand on the small of her back. He led her into a wide living room with no furniture. Just a big open space with gorgeous wood floors. The kind of place where she could imagine kids running around and big family meals on a long table with everyone talking and passing dishes. The kind of upbringing she and Gage hadn't had.

"What do you say?" He grinned.

She turned to look at him. "About what?"

"Starting a family." He dug in his pocket and produced a ring. Gold, with a huge diamond. "Apparently this was your grandmother's, and it's a family heirloom. Your mother *insisted*." He shrugged. "I figure if you don't want to wear it all the time, I can get you something more everyday wearable, and you can do whatever you want."

Clare studied him. "And what do you want?"

"You." Gage waited a beat, then said, "It's always been you."

She had to agree with that. "Same."

He smiled and tugged her close, the ring in his hand now behind her back. "I've always loved you."

She dropped the crutches and slid her hands behind his neck. "Probably kind of like the way I've always loved you. Even when I didn't want to."

"Good. Hang on to that, because you'll probably need it."

Clare smiled.

Gage tugged her close and kissed her, the way she'd always loved. Putting the missing pieces of her life back together in a way only he could.

She'd read a verse in the Bible about that recently, about how God restored years eaten by locusts. Which, honestly, felt like pretty much her whole life.

All she'd had for years was dryness. Famine. Gage was the rain that watered everything, and God used him to restore new life in her. Even after God had given her so much, there was Gage. An extra blessing on top of everything.

He pulled back. "Marry me."

Clare's hands squeezed reflexively on his shoulders. "Yes."

He kissed her again and slid the ridiculous ring onto her finger. "We can decide about the house later."

"I already know I love it. And it'll be wonderful for the McCauleys to know they gave you this."

Gage nodded. "Thank you."

She had no idea why he was thanking her, but she kissed him anyway. Her life had changed so much in the last few weeks her head was still spinning. Gage swept her up with everything he was, and she'd told him so many times how amazing he was that he'd told her to stop. Which only made her feel like he was even more amazing. Especially when he blushed.

Something he was doing right now.

He touched his forehead to hers. "We need to go outside. Everyone is waiting."

"What?" She had to laugh.

Gage grabbed her crutches and led her through the open kitchen, giving her zero time to look at the backsplash and appreciate the light fixtures. The counters were covered with bags and containers. A cooler had been stacked on another cooler, tucked against the wall.

"What's going on?"

He stepped out the patio door, and she saw tables over the lawn. People hanging out. Cops. Vanguard staff. Three grills had been lined up in a row, and Bob Davis held court. He had a few cops around him, and FBI agents from town, plus friends she knew from out of town.

"Are we having a party?"

Gage glanced at her, a sheepish look on his face. "An engagement party. Your mom insisted."

Clare burst out laughing. "This backyard is gorgeous. Let's get married out here."

"Soon." Gage tugged her over and kissed her again. Then he turned to the crowd of people and yelled, "She said yes!"

A chorus of cheers erupted across the lawn.

Clare hoped she heard that sound a lot, for the rest of her life. The sound her heart made when she considered the love of God.

And a good man she'd always loved.

I really hope you enjoyed *Collateral*, would you please consider leaving a review? It really helps others find their next read.

The saga continues with *Detection* releasing in Summer 2023. Find out more about it and the Benson First Responders series at my website series page: https://authorlisaphillips.com/benson-first-responders

If you haven't already subscribed to my newsletter, swing by and sign up today to stay informed on new releases and promotions. New Subscribers also get stuff! https://authorlisaphillips.com/subscribe

ALSO BY LISA PHILLIPS

Find out more about Benson First Responders on the series page:

https://authorlisaphillips.com/benson-first-responders

Benson First Responders is a continuation of Last Chance Downrange. Read the whole Last Chance Downrange series now!

Point of Impact - Available in AUDIO Dec 15, 2022!

Hard Target - Available in AUDIO Jan 2023!

Hollow Point - Coming to Audio in 2023!

Terminal Velocity - Coming to Audio in 2023!

Audio Available from Podium Publishing

Find more stories based in Last Chance County at:

www.lastchancecounty.com

Last Chance Website

Other series by Lisa:

Brand of Justice (Thriller series - New for 2022!)

Benson First Responders (Christian Romantic Suspense - New for 2022!)

Chevalier Protection Specialists

Last Chance County

Northwest Counter-Terrorism Taskforce

Double Down

WITSEC Town (Sanctuary)

And numerous other titles including several from Love Inspired Suspense.

Find the complete list here:

https://authorlisaphillips.com/full-book-list

Full Book List

ABOUT THE AUTHOR

Find out more about Lisa Phillips at her website:
https://authorlisaphillips.com/about-the-author

Learn about Lisa's work with Sunrise Publishing at:
https://sunrisepublishing.com/author-lisa-phillips/

Would you also share about the book on Social Media, leave a review on Lisa's page and share about your experience? Your review will help others find great clean fiction and decide what to read next!

Scan the QR below to sign up for Lisa's newsletter and don't forget to follow her on social media!

Made in the USA
Middletown, DE
11 January 2025

69322593R00156